DJIBI

Also by Felix Salten

Bambi
Bambi's Children
Renni the Rescuer
A Forest World
The Hound of Florence
The City Jungle
Fifteen Rabbits
Florian
Perri

DJIBI

BAMBI'S CLASSIC ANIMAL TALES

FELIX SALTEN
Translated by RAYA LEVIN

Aladdin
New York   London   Toronto   Sydney   New Delhi

ALADDIN

An imprint of Simon & Schuster Children's Publishing Division
1230 Avenue of the Americas, New York, New York 10020
This Aladdin paperback edition February 2016
Text copyright © 1945 by Albert Müller Verlag
English language translation copyright © 1948 by Julian Messner, Inc.
Originally published in German in 1945 by Albert Müller Verlag as *Djibi, das Kätzchen.*
Cover illustration copyright © 2016 by Richard Cowdrey
Also available in an Aladdin hardcover edition.
All rights reserved, including the right of reproduction
in whole or in part in any form.
ALADDIN is a trademark of Simon & Schuster, Inc., and related
logo is a registered trademark of Simon & Schuster, Inc.
For information about special discounts for bulk purchases, please contact
Simon & Schuster Special Sales at 1-866-506-1949 or business@simonandschuster.com.
The Simon & Schuster Speakers Bureau can bring authors to your live
event. For more information or to book an event contact the Simon & Schuster
Speakers Bureau at 1-866-248-3049 or visit our website at www.simonspeakers.com.
Cover designed by Karin Paprocki
Interior designed by Hilary Zarycky
The text of this book was set in Yana.
Manufactured in the United States of America 0116 OFF
2 4 6 8 10 9 7 5 3 1
Library of Congress Control Number 2015936613
ISBN 978-1-4424-8765-9 (hc)
ISBN 978-1-4424-8764-2 (pbk)
ISBN 978-1-4424-8766-6 (eBook)

DJIBI

I.

SPLASH!

The young little kitten, thrown by a rough hand, flew into the water. She had barely opened her eyes, when an attempt was already made to deny life to her.

Three of the kittens had been drowned as soon as they were born. The remaining three were left with their mother, feeling cozy and warm, and enjoying her milk, until a brutal voice cried: "Two are enough!"

The young kitten heard this thundering voice, but, of course, she understood nothing.

She was grabbed and hurled into the pond.

Splash!

Her tender body felt the hard grip with a painful shock. The fall dazed her small brain, but contact with the water revived her sufficiently to experience all the horror and torment of the wet cold.

The little creature, yielding weakly, was now carried along by the waves. She was unconscious, and felt only the hostile, cold water. Dizziness clouded her confused senses, and she touched the shore several times without realizing it.

The small boy who fished the wretched creature out cried: "A kitten!"

Compassionately he laid the rescued kitten next to him on a warm, sunny stone.

"Is the poor thing still alive?" The poor thing was alive. She breathed feebly, but she breathed.

Lying there exhausted, ill-treated, nearly dead, she was a touching sight.

The boy's heart swelled with pity. For a long time he sat at the side of the miserable kitten and watched her in silence, and began to love her innocent grace with all the stormy intensity of a child's heart.

At last she began to whimper softly. Very, very softly.

Her dark gray fur, with its black tiger stripes, was drying quickly in the sun, and the reviving warmth penetrated deeply into the kitten's body. The tiny snout opened softly, and a faint, though now audible, plaintive sound emerged. It was a thin, pitiful wail, but the boy was pleased about it, almost happy. He picked the little thing up very carefully, pressed her to his heart, and carried her home.

The soft voice remained silent for a moment, but then complained no longer, but purred sweetly and melodiously.

"I'll tell you what," said the mother to the boy. "Take her to Lady in the stable. She has two puppies. Put the kitten to her breast. If she sucks, all will be well."

"But Lady . . . will she let her?"

The mother smiled. "Don't worry. Just try."

Lady, the big Alsatian, was puzzled when the kitten was brought to her. But two of her puppies had been taken away, and she accepted the newcomer willingly.

She immediately began to treat the stranger as her own offspring, licking the kitten's fur with her warm tongue.

The latter felt quite at home, nestled in between the two puppies till she reached the motherly breast, and drank greedily, as though parched with thirst.

The boy stood proudly by. He had saved the little creature's life.

The stable was plunged in semidarkness, and a pleasant, milky odor floated in the air.

Five cows stood there, stamping their feet, whipping their flanks with their tails to chase away the flies. The smacking sounds repeated themselves at irregular intervals. From time to time one or the other of the cows would emit a grunt, almost like a deep sigh.

Quite apart from the cows, separated from them by a special box, stood the bull. His hide was uniformly black and carefully brushed. A nose-ring kept his boundless strength under control. He had a white spot on his breast. His breath often blew like a loud snort.

Actually he was quite a mild bull; the farmer loved him and took him daily for a walk. Every day at the same time the farmer would come into the stable and the bull would follow him obediently on their usual walk.

The kitten grew and grew, unconcerned at the proximity of such mighty creatures.

On his way to the bull, the farmer, followed by the boy, who was his son, stopped at the dog basket.

"There is an example of kind motherhood for you!"

"You're thinking of the kitten, Father? Do you think she'll turn out well?"

"How should I know? A cat is always a gamble. But I hope so. If the little thing is going to live, she must have a name."

"A name, Father? I'll think about it."

"Think, my boy. Thinking never does any harm."

The farmer approached the bull, who greeted him with loud snorting and impatient stamping.

"Come on, Peter, come now. The two of us are going on a ramble."

The farmer loosened the rope which fastened the nose-ring to the trough. The bull turned round immediately and marched out of the stable with a stilted step, while the farmer gently patted his back.

Deep affection stirred in the man's heart.

The man and the bull walked along the village road like two comrades. The man chatted ceaselessly. The bull nodded his massive skull as though in approval and wagged his thick ears all the time.

After about an hour the farmer said: "It's time to go home, Peter." The black giant obeyed without demur, quietly allowed himself to be tied back to his stable and submitted to the vigorous caresses and pattings which sent quivering jerks all along his body.

Days followed days. Weeks passed by. Everything remained peacefully the same: the milking of the cows, which was done by the farmer's wife, the brushing and exercising of the bull.

The kitten was far in advance of her foster brothers. The two puppies were still toddling, plump and awkward, when she could already dance gracefully and vivaciously round her foster mother, jump in and out of the basket and explore all the corners of the stable. When the boy lifted and caressed her, she purred loudly. He whispered tenderly: "Djibi, my Djibi . . ."

But she wanted to be free, and wriggled until he put her down again.

Everyone was delighted with the little thing's intelligence.

Her two foster brothers, however, showed her no great affection; they provoked her constantly, but when they became too rough, she knew how to use her sharp claws in a most painful manner.

Djibi was soon at home not only throughout the stable—and made sure that she always got her fair share of milk at milking time—but also found her way into the farmer's living room and kitchen.

When she saw a piece of string dangling down from the table, after a parcel had been opened, she tried to catch it with her paws; she raised herself in the attempt, and chased it eagerly and gaily. The swinging movements of the string were a game to her, specially intended for her amusement–that was how she treated everything that lent itself to play.

The boy laughed, the mother laughed, the father smiled. Djibi's dancing grace won her applause and affection.

The boy got out a top and spun it round.

Djibi was taken aback; for a time she looked on with her little head cocked to one side, but suddenly she jumped up and bravely hit out with her paw. The top lay vanquished and motionless. Djibi watched it anxiously, prowled round it and pawed it gently.

Every one of her gestures was charming, she was a source of gaiety and carefree jolliness.

She was extremely particular as regards cleanliness; she cleaned herself elaborately and at great length, and when she grew tired, she always chose the same spot in front of the stove. She slept there for several hours during the day and sometimes at night. Comfortably stretched out, she began to purr as soon as the boy came in to stroke her. He always liked it, and he thought how he had fished her out of the water, half dead, and how bright she was now. He was pleased with his rescue work and woke the kitten, who was never too tired to play.

In the stable she often felt lonely. Then she would hop fearlessly among the cows, who occasionally sniffed at her. Even the bull tolerated her, and snorted at her good-naturedly. Mostly she indulged in terrific fights with her foster brothers, only in fun, of course. Lady, the puppies' mother, now walked about in the court-yard.

One day, Djibi had the opportunity of showing that she was useful as well as amusing.

She was sitting alone in the kitchen, blinking idly, when a poor mouse, suspecting no danger, ventured out of her hole to get a tidbit, and was suddenly confronted with her worst enemy.

Bad luck!

In her terror, utterly confused and panic-stricken, not knowing where to escape, the mouse ran up the wall. Thereby she came even more clearly into the field of vision of Djibi, who had already cocked her ears at the first rustling sound.

A mouse for the first time! Djibi was nonplussed. But her eyes sparkled!

The mouse was so annihilated by this terrible look that she was quite unable to move or flee. This strange spell lasted for two long seconds.

Then Djibi simply caught hold of the mouse with her teeth, shook the numb creature vigorously, and put her down on the floor. This was a sudden idea.

Bleeding, almost unconscious, dizzy, the mouse realized the impossibility of escape and submitted helplessly to her fate. Nevertheless, she ran a few tiny steps, almost as though to oblige the cat.

Djibi followed every movement with her head cocked, hit out again at the bleeding creature.

The mouse still moved on, was stopped again, ran

painfully for the third time and then remained motionless under Djibi's claws—her last breath of life had
expired.

Djibi still pushed the small body about. The cruel
game had not lasted long enough for her.

At last she carried the dead mouse into the living
room and laid her booty proudly on a chair.

"Look, Mother, what Djibi has brought," cried the boy.

"Look, Father!" said the farmer's wife.

"Good, Djibi. Very good!" praised the farmer.

"That's right!" his wife agreed, while the boy pressed
Djibi to his heart and caressed her. Djibi showed her
delight by prolonged purring.

From now on Djibi knew no greater pleasure than
chasing mice. She lay in wait for them in dark corners,
searched for them in the house, in the stable, kept a jealous watch over the larder. She was not hungry, and ate
the mice only as a reward. But her passion for hunting
was never satisfied.

Djibi spent many happy weeks in this manner.

In the stable she had friendly tussles with the dogs.

Like Djibi, they had grown up, but were much bigger and surpassed her both in size and strength. Nevertheless, Djibi's agility had the better of them. She never allowed herself to be hurt. Sometimes when she got hurt, even if only by accident, she would punish the clumsy offender by boxing his ears vigorously, whereupon he would withdraw in confusion.

Djibi lived her own life gaily, enjoying her milk, and as she was solely concerned with her own welfare, she did not notice the mood of depression that had descended upon the household.

The farmer was sad, and so was his wife; the boy, too, seemed subdued. The veterinary surgeon had said that the bull was ill beyond cure, and would die soon.

Djibi knew nothing of all this. She took no notice of human sorrow. She hardly even noticed that for days on end the boy omitted to take her into his arms and caress her. When she wanted to be petted, she jumped up to his chest and shoulder and poked her pretty head under his chin, purring loudly. He would then stroke her fur, but only for a short moment, and then put her down on the floor. But Djibi was quite satisfied with even a short game.

One day, at dawn, the bull was found dead in his box. He had grown thin as a skeleton and was lying on his side, his eyes shut, as though asleep.

The vet was called, but he only shrugged his shoulders: "I told you a long time ago that you ought to put an end to the beast."

But the farmer, disconsolate, refused to move from the dead bull's side. He was so shaken that he was unable to utter a word.

His wife sobbed heartbreakingly. She was worried over the material damage caused by the loss of the bull, and grieved over her husband's sorrow.

The boy ran howling out of the stable. But because he was hungry, he ran into the kitchen.

There a decisive scene took place between him and Djibi.

Djibi meant no harm when she hastened to meet him and tried to jump on his shoulder as usual.

But the boy pushed her back: "Leave me alone!"

Djibi made a second attempt at re-establishing their long-standing intimacy. At the first sign of her intention, however, the boy cried:

"Leave me alone, you damned beast!" At the same time he slapped the cat's head with impatient indignation.

A slap? Djibi never accepted a slap without retaliation, never!

As quick as lightning, her sharp claws dug into the boy's hand, from which a few drops of blood began to trickle. He staggered back in pain, while the cat, spitting, sat up on her hind legs and raised her paws in readiness for both defense and attack.

The boy did not remember that he had pulled Djibi out of the water and saved her poor little life; he did not remember how often she had amused and delighted him. At the moment she appeared to him as a wild, excited enemy, and he was her exasperated, badly scratched opponent.

It never occurred to him that he was responsible for this sudden transformation. Embittered, he reached out for the cat, to throw her against the wall, to punish her. To show her who was master.

But Djibi admitted no punishment. The very notion of it, so well known to dogs, was completely alien to her.

She submitted to neither ill-treatment nor to punishment. Nothing of the kind!

She had suffered gross unfairness, never gave a thought to the past, or to her once beloved friend. She had finished with him forever.

In the face of his angry attitude, she ran stealthily past him, and jumped out of the window before he had realized it.

Into freedom!

II.

DJIBI RAN FAR AWAY. THE FIELDS stretched wide in front of her. She ran, whipping her flanks with her tail. Somewhere in a cornfield she sat down. She was still very excited, and her tail end jerked to and fro.

The corn was already quite tall, and hid her like a dense forest.

Soon she grew calmer, and immediately proceeded to attend to her toilet.

Her tongue carefully washed her breast, tummy and almost the whole of her back. Her paws went over her face. She licked them and they returned again and again to clean her face and ears.

At last she was satisfied. The quarrel and her former home were almost forgotten. At any rate she didn't bother about it. She had her freedom, and that seemed to her all she could desire.

After a while she felt hungry. Greedily she fell over every beetle which came her way, but these were only mouthfuls, certainly not enough to make a meal.

Cautiously she crept along, sniffing the air in search of prey.

A little bird fluttered up in agitation. A lark anxious for her brood.

Djibi's attention was arrested. She did not take her eyes off the lark. The unfortunate bird led her unwittingly to her nest, which lay flat and unprotected on the ground. Four half-fledged chicks touchingly opened their beaks.

But Djibi knew no mercy and ate up all four chicks,

one after the other. The feeble squeaks of her victims, the impotent fluttering of the mother, only increased Djibi's pleasure in her prey.

Then two field mice fell victim to her.

She started in surprise when a pheasant flew up in her close vicinity, his wings rattling loudly. Djibi was fascinated by the scintillating display of the colored plumage, and attracted by the size of the bird. She would have liked to get hold of him. Yes, he would still her hunger.

She lay in wait, trying to catch a pheasant. But, however sly her maneuvers, she did not succeed. Here and there a bird would flutter up with an alarming noise. Djibi darted to and fro across the field, but came always too late and all her efforts were in vain.

In days to come, Djibi was destined to catch as many pheasants as she wanted with the greatest of ease, but of this she had at present no inkling. A quail, which she caught instead, was but a poor substitute for the large coveted birds.

She crossed the cornfield and came into the open onto a wide, sunny footpath. Djibi felt the glowing heat of the sun as a caress. She stretched herself comfortably on the grass border and dozed pleasantly.

She was no longer tormented by hunger, nor tempted into a strenuous chase by alluring pheasants. The smells of the earth and the fields, of mice and other prey caressed her nostrils. She felt completely happy, carefree and at ease.

But danger and adventure were not far off.

A man came along, preceded by a frisky, attractive and bristling fox terrier.

A dog! Djibi had always maintained a staunch friendship with the dogs on the farm. She sat up confidently and awaited the arrival of her new playmate with a pleasant sense of eagerness.

She did not hear the man's inciting words: "Go for the cat! Get her!" Nor would she have understood them.

The fox terrier stormed at her; Djibi was thrown over so violently that she rolled down the bank. She considered this as a rather rough game, but still a game.

The terrier followed her, was close at her heels, and then fell over her.

Only now did she recognize the enemy at his furious bark and sharp teeth, which snapped mercilessly at
her and, on one occasion, even tore painfully into her
flesh. She disentangled herself from the attacker's grip
with great agility and faced him, hissing with hatred.
The terrier tried to get at her again, but a well-aimed
blow at his muzzle sent him reeling back.

Djibi hit out at him again and again, always aiming
at his eyes. He turned right and left to avoid her blows,
waiting for a propitious moment to take his revenge.
But Djibi's claws tore bleeding streaks into his forehead,
and he howled in agony.

The man tried to intervene with his stick and come
to the rescue of his dog, but at that moment Djibi took
to her heels. She fled into a cornfield and disappeared
among the swaying blades.

The dog lacked the courage to follow her.

Djibi was well sheltered.

She strolled about aimlessly, excited and out of
breath. It was a long time before she grew calm again
and settled down to her toilet.

She reflected upon her recent experience. Dogs were by no means harmless playmates and good comrades, but enemies! One had to be careful on encountering a dog. The best policy was immediate flight, or a merciless battle if it could not be avoided. At last, very tired, Djibi fell asleep.

But suddenly she was torn out of her slumber. She felt pangs of hunger, but suppressed them, because she had been awakened by a sharp acrid smell which penetrated into her nostrils.

Djibi was immediately on her guard. She arched her back and surveyed the scene intently.

A fox was gingerly picking his way through the corn, hunting for mice.

Djibi and the fox faced each other with surprise. She took him for a dog, having never seen a fox before. She spat menacingly, ready for a fight.

The fox pounced at her, and a wave of his overwhelming smell hit Djibi in the face. She very nearly fainted.

Fear assailed her now. At her wits' end, she jumped

over the fox, and ran, with a single thought in her mind. Flight! She dared not stand her ground against this enemy. She ran as though possessed, driven by a deadly fear. This was by no means a dog. He was a dangerous savage, a dreadful, terrifying stranger.

She heard the corn rustle behind her. The stranger was pursuing her. Both came out of the field into the open. A wide road stretched in front of Djibi, leading to a wood.

Djibi hastily climbed up the nearest tree, a mighty beech. Hidden in the leafy top, she peered down.

If the dangerous enemy could also climb, what then? But the fox leaned against the trunk with his front legs and grunted impotently.

Djibi felt safe.

The wide branch on which she was sitting offered her slender body a cozy resting place. She enjoyed a prolonged spell of quiet relaxation. It took some time before she felt able to tidy herself, but eventually she did, and very thoroughly, too.

She then kept a close watch on her surroundings.

Her hunting instincts were roused with her growing hunger.

Various birds flew in and out of the green thicket. Djibi snatched at them with her paws, but her attempts were feeble and unsuccessful. A jay escaped her, and uttered an angry, screeching cry. The sparrows met her antics with derisive laughter. The finches and robins never came near her and were far too quick, anyway.

A squirrel darted by, nimble, gay, amiable.

All Djibi's hunting lust flared up. She ducked and waited.

Without a doubt there were many tasty tidbits up in the sheltering treetops! Djibi did not move. Only the end of her tail was quivering. She could not suppress it.

The squirrel came dancing back. He did not notice the cat, and crouched down gracefully, pressing his short little paws to his white breast.

The lovely, candid creature had barely time to be frightened, let alone to escape. A very short squeak, and bright red blood came trickling down from his gaping throat.

Djibi had now satisfied her ravenous hunger. Feeling better, she began to prowl through the branches.

With the falling night she grew still bolder, and became doubly enterprising.

Now the birds sat in their nests, surrendering themselves to the peace of the night, lapsing into that state of beatitude in which they could be overpowered without a chance of fluttering away.

Djibi made the wicked resolution to attack the sleeping birds and devour them in turn.

An ear-splitting crowing startled her. She stood motionless, listening. The crowing fascinated her, and was accompanied by a loud clatter of wings.

The pheasants!

Djibi had not yet grasped what was happening. But she did not move, listened attentively with a quivering tail, and licked her chops, full of anticipation.

Again the clatter of wings.

At last Djibi understood. The pheasants were flying to their homesteads in the trees.

A great joy filled Djibi's heart.

She sat down comfortably and waited.

Let it grow quite dark first, pitch black—she would then go out in search of the pheasants, and catch one of them right in his sleep.

A pheasant!

The unknown, horrid enemy, who had chased her into the wood and up the trees, would never reach her here.

Djibi was triumphant.

Had she known the meaning of gratitude, she would have been grateful to him. As is was, she only sneered at him secretly.

There she was, extending her rule over many pheasants and squirrels, which were living there in great numbers. An owl flew past noiselessly; Djibi heard her melancholy song only later.

She started when a wood-owl broke into a piercing shriek next to her. The sounds of the nocturnal forest, strange and weird, were to her like the voice of an unknown, mysterious life, which whispered, muttered and rustled all round her, on the ground below, among the branches above. She sat and listened, pricked her ears and slowly regained her confidence.

She heard, at first very near her, the lamenting song of the owl, which slowly receded into the distance. Then she saw the wood owl, who was balancing on a branch not far off; but his cries, however shrill, did not frighten Djibi any more.

She remembered the pheasants, and the thought of surprising them in their sleep made her feel feverish.

Djibi began to look for this prey, for which she felt such a strong desire.

Silently she crept from tree to tree, passing several pheasants on her way without noticing or recognising them. Suddenly she almost collided with one, perched soundly asleep on a branch, with his head buried beneath his wing. She inhaled the warm smell of his body, which seemed larger than she had imagined. A bite, and the warm blood poured over her face.

There was no defense, no fluttering, hardly a quiver. The pheasant had slipped from slumber into death, and knew nothing of the end.

Djibi pulled her prey to pieces, devoured it at first greedily and in haste, afterward more leisurely, having had her fill with one half of the bird, at last only out of gourmandise, until she could eat no more.

There was still quite a lot left of her victim. Djibi left the remains and dragged herself away from the scene of her crime, utterly replete, looking for a resting place, which she found in the thickly grown summit of a tall old plane tree.

The morning dawned. The awakening forest resounded with the sweet song of the blackbird, the jubilant stanzas of the finch and the robin, the whispers of the titmouse, the loud chatting of the magpie, the joyful shouts of the oriole, the crowing of the rook.

Djibi heard nothing of all that.

She lay fast asleep, and slept most of the day.

The crows and the blackbirds had discovered the remains of the pheasant, gathered round to have a meal, quarreled and fought over their shares until nothing was left of the dead bird but the feathers to bear evidence of the murder.

The forest-keeper passed by later on, accompanied by the gamekeeper.

He saw the traces and said: "Some bird of prey, or possibly a marten, has killed a pheasant."

"I'll keep a lookout!" said the gamekeeper.

Djibi slept and remained invisible.

Toward the evening she woke up, fresh, alert, eager for her hunt, because she was hungry. Soon she could hear the crowing of the rising pheasants, the clatter of their wings.

Djibi did not move from her place.

She was assured of a pheasant tonight. She knew it and waited.

In complete darkness she prowled through the trees, light-footed, stalked up to the dark clump, now familiar to her.

For a short while she sat near the pheasant on which her choice had fallen, enjoying the pleasure of the attack in anticipation. Then came the quick, deadly bite, the surging blood which poured hotly over her, and finally the sumptuous, leisurely meal in complete security.

This time, too, she could only consume part of the pheasant.

Satiated, over-full, she made her way back, crawling lazily to her plane tree, which was some distance from the pheasants' refuge. She then proceeded to clean her face and breast very thoroughly, and went to sleep before daybreak.

From now on she slayed a pheasant night after night, and slept throughout the day.

The moon rose in the starry sky, at first a narrow sickle, then half, and finally the forest was lit up by the full moon.

Djibi was just about to pounce on her victim when a shot burst out. It seemed like the cracking of a whip, a sound known to Djibi from the farm.

Djibi had been spotted by the gamekeeper. Though he could not see her clearly, he knew that he was in the presence of a beast of prey, responsible for the death of many a pheasant.

He fired.

Djibi was hit in the thigh. She vanished like lightning.

But she could not run for very long because the small wound was burning like fire.

Djibi limped to her plane tree, pulling up her injured leg.

That the first shot she heard should have been aimed at her! A cold terror shook her. Dare she go hunting again?

For the present, however, she had neither the strength nor the inclination to pursue her prey.

She crouched woefully on her branch, licking her wound over and over again.

It never occurred to her that she had escaped death; she was only filled by a bitter feeling of being singled out for misfortunes.

The pain subsided, but she was even more tormented by fear. Her heart sank at the thought of the lurking danger. The pheasants were safe from her. Forever.

She could find no sleep, and her stirring hunger was suppressed by her nervous agitation and her feeling of utter hopelessness.

In the dead of night a sniffing creature approached Djibi, stopping irresolutely in front of her.

The marten.

He hesitated whether to attack her or to make a friendly advance.

Djibi did not await his decision.

She spat furiously and raised her front paws menacingly.

The marten was surprised. He had not seen such an animal in the vicinity.

"Where do you come from?"

"It's none of your business!"

"Why so cross?"

"I've got a pain!"

"Where?"

"Here!" Djibi showed her wound. "A shot!"

"Ah! The hand of fire?"

"Hand of fire? What nonsense!"

"But I know it! He has a hand of fire."

"Don't talk such rubbish. The man had a gun!"

"Call it a gun if you like . . ."

"Oh course! I know the two-legged creatures well. I've been with them for a long time."

"Tell me! What are they like?"

"Sometimes quite nice. But generally bad, very bad!"

"Here in the forest they are only bad, always! And terribly dangerous!"

"I've got proof of that!" Djibi raised her wounded thigh. "This shot . . ."

"Of the hand of fire . . ."

"Of the gun . . ."

"Was aimed at me!"

Djibi contradicted. "No, at me!"

"You're wrong! At me," insisted the marten.

"No!" Djibi grew excited. "No! At me!"

"I tell you, he was aiming at me!"

"Anyhow, he hit me, not you!"

"I'm sorry, but he meant to hit me."

"No, me. Only me!"

The marten abandoned the argument. "Yes, these full moon nights . . . we have to be very careful."

"I am not so well acquainted with the forest, not so experienced . . ."

"You'll learn!"

Djibi, convulsed with pain, wailed: "Learn! If I don't starve in the meantime!"

"One does not starve so easily."

"Bring me something to eat! Anything," begged Djibi.

The marten grinned. "I bring you something? Have you an idea of my own hunger, my own thirst for blood?"

"You wretched fellow!"

"On a shooting night like this, I'm thankful if I can get something for myself," apologized the marten. He added: "It's lucky for you I don't strangle you!"

"Lucky!" hissed Djibi, wildly. "You just try it, just try!" In her fury she raised her claws, forgot her pain and prepared to scratch the marten's eyes out.

"I'll have no dealings with you," muttered the marten, turned on his heels and disappeared noiselessly.

Djibi was left alone with her troubles; she suffered great pain, pangs of hunger and fear.

She did not quite know what she was afraid of, but it was precisely this fear of the unknown which tormented her most.

She grew rapidly thin, she who until now had always been thriving well.

But her wound healed gradually, so that she was able to get up and search for food. Her thigh, however, remained stiff, and she limped. It also remained sensitive, as though remembering past pains.

She had to be content with small prey. As quick as lightning she would fall over any creature she could spy or reach. She was not driven by hunger alone; anger was mingled with her hunger, as though she wanted to take some revenge, some bloody retaliation.

She played cruelly with her victims, gloated over the death struggle of the magpies, jays, sparrows or squirrels, before she decided to put an end to their tortures.

Suddenly, Djibi noticed that the trees were shedding their leaves.

Autumn had come.

She paid no attention to the roaring and the fighting

of the deer. But the falling leaves rustled through the forest like a mysterious whisper and filled her with anxiety.

The nights were cold. Djibi shivered—she could never stand the cold.

One day an icy storm blew through the wood, sweeping the leaves into whirling columns.

The plane tree soon lost all its foliage, and the other trees, too, were standing bare.

Djibi had to descend to the ground.

She did so one pitch-black night, and crawled into the bushes.

At dawn she caught a rabbit, and had a meal which revived her strength. She went to sleep afterward, but could not regain her former carefree frame of mind. She frequently changed her abode, and was handicapped by her lame thigh. She was in constant fear of meeting her evil enemy, the fox, and was also haunted by other fears.

The cold and the shortage of food at last drove Djibi to the resolution to turn to the two-legged creatures in quest of shelter and refuge.

The first house she reached was that of the forest-keeper, but she was chased away by the dogs, and the forest-keeper reached for his gun to fire at the cat.

Djibi fled into the nearest copse, and clawed the dog who pursued her until his eyes were blinded by blood and he retreated in confusion. She then began a cautious investigation of the forest, which seemed endless, starting nervously at every real or imaginary danger-signal.

During that time she lived frugally on an occasional mouse, and slept restlessly only when exhausted by utter fatigue.

At last, she came into the open.

Wide stubble fields stretched in front of her. In the distance she could see the smoking chimneys of the village cottages.

Djibi cowered in the furrows, waited, hoped, worried and hoped again.

When two men passed by, she limped toward them, whimpering desolately.

One of them stopped and picked her up. "Come, poor pussy!" he said.

Djibi was seduced by the soft sound of his voice. She nestled in his breast and purred loudly, enchanted by the warmth of his body. She had reached her goal at last! She heard the two men talking to each other, but, of course, did not understand a word of their conversation. She continued to purr, and the man was stroking her.

"Can you hear her?" he asked his companion.

"I'm not deaf!" the other replied gruffly.

The man let the unfriendly answer pass.

"Do you know what this purring means?"

"Perhaps gratitude?" sneered the other.

"You may call it gratitude; it is, at any rate, a sign of confidence."

"She purrs because she feels comfortable . . . it's entirely selfish."

The man was a schoolteacher in a fairly large hamlet, and his companion a farmer.

"Selfishness is her right," the teacher smiled. "Every living being has a right to self-preservation."

"My dog is not selfish," replied the farmer.

"He is! But in an entirely different manner to this cat."

"I would really like to know how you can say that my dog..."

"Do you ever beat him?"

"Of course! When he deserves it!"

"There you are! Your dog does his best to avoid a beating. From an instinct of self-preservation!"

"No! Out of obedience, faithfulness..."

"I admit it, dogs are obedient and faithful... because that is how they can make things easier for themselves."

"Only for that reason?"

"No. They love human beings. Their master is their God."

"Isn't that fine?"

"Of course it is! Of course!"

"But cats are false and malicious! Do you agree?"

"By no means!"

"Do you believe you'll ever become this cat's master?"

"I'll be glad to become her friend."

"Its sheer nonsense, all this going on over a stray cat!"

"In your view, perhaps!"

"In the view of all reasonable people!"

"In your view, then, I am unreasonable?"

"As regards cats, you're a . . ."

"A fool?"

"I never meant to say that, Teacher! You're exaggerating again; you always are!"

They reached the village and parted company.

"I'll be curious to know," called the farmer after the teacher, "how your dog will take to this cat!"

Without answering, the teacher went into his house.

"Look what I've got!" he said as he put Djibi down. Tasso, the Airedale dog, rushed at him.

Djibi arched her back and spat. But she soon gained confidence, because the large dog sniffed at her in a friendly manner. He had brown and steel-gray fur, a round head with tousled hair, and his jaws were full of sharp teeth which could bite with lightning speed and disastrous consequences. Any dog, however vicious, who attacked him, would roll in his blood after a brief fight and be compelled to run away. But Tasso pursued no one. He was always peaceable, knew no vengeance, no hatred.

Djibi now went round and round this dangerous giant, her tail standing up rigidly.

Tasso only had a stump, which he wagged slightly.

"The enmity between dogs and cats," said the teacher to his wife, "is partly due to jealousy, and partly to human incitement which for generations has been driving these animals against each other."

"Maybe," replied Bertha, his wife, "perhaps you're right, but that is of very little interest to me at the moment. The cat is more than half-starved!" She placed a bowl of milk on the floor. Djibi drank, delighted and greedy. She had not tasted anything like it for a long time.

Tasso looked on pleasantly, as though he were the host.

Then Djibi glanced round the room. She saw a mat lying by the stove; it was Tasso's place. She made straight for it, lay down and immediately sank into the deep sleep of exhaustion.

Now Djibi had a home again as before. No longer

any need to worry over food, to fear the hand of fire.

Her relations with Tasso were excellent; she domineered him, and he even suffered her to tyrannize him.

The farmer, with whom the teacher had been talking when he carried Djibi home in his arms, called one day.

He saw the way Djibi carried on with Tasso and was indignant.

"Why do you dislike cats so much?" asked the teacher.

"I've told you before," replied the farmer, "I dislike them because they are false and vicious."

"You're mistaken! You must not misunderstand them."

"How do you mean, 'misunderstand them'? I know the creatures far better than you do!"

"I should doubt it very much."

"Well, prove to me that this cat obeys you! Then you'll convince me that I'm wrong."

"Do you require every animal to be obedient?"

"Naturally it must obey, if it is to live under my roof!"

"That's it, my friend. I never demand obedience. My Tasso obeys me voluntarily. It is a quality his race has had for thousands of years. Pussy knows no obedience, and therein precisely lies her charm—to me, at least."

"A strange charm!"

"You see, the cat is a free being! If you like, it is a wild beast, untamed and untamable. She has noble relations, the lions, tigers, leopards . . ."

"Yes! and these are wisely kept behind bars, in strong cages!"

"Men are cruel enough to do this to them."

"What else do you suggest should be done with them?"

"They should either be left at liberty, or shot."

"You're funny, Teacher!"

"Perhaps! I'm funny enough to be opposed to the so-called taming of wild animals."

"Why do you say 'so-called'?"

"Because I don't believe there is such a thing as real taming! I can only believe in the fear and the torments endured by the unfortunate captive lions and tigers. I am foolish enough to disbelieve those enthusiastic tamers who pretend that a tiger is happiest in captivity.

These beasts adapt themselves and are grateful if one is kind to them, just like the domestic cat."

"Give me one good reason for this strange love of yours."

"One? As many as you like!"

"One will do, but it must be a good one."

"The cat is free, she is independent, and stays with human beings only for her own convenience."

"I said a *good* reason, Teacher!"

"Her precious sincerity!"

"But cats are false, Teacher, false and vicious!"

"Be reasonable, Farmer! Be nice to a cat, and you will win her friendship."

"Do you mean that I, a man, should be on my best behavior to be honored by a cat's friendship?"

"That's what I do mean."

"You're not quite right in the head, Teacher!"

"Possibly not. But you see, I have no pretentions. Most people imagine that animals exist for the sole purpose of serving them."

"That's as it should be!"

"Not at all! If nature had her way, even hens and doves would grow wild!"

"That is quite possible."

"There you are! The cat is as nature meant her to be. She does not have to grow wild first. She is and remains a wild animal!"

"And that is what you respect?"

"Very much so! Leave her alone, and she will be gentle. Be kind to her—I'll say it again—and she will grow to like you. Once you have gotten that far you may well be proud!"

"You are determined to stick to your madness, Teacher?"

"If kindness, trust, and gentleness are madness in your eyes, I am!"

"Tell me what reward you get for your kindness and confidence?"

"Remember, kindness and trust always earn us a good reward from our dumb friends."

"From the cat as well?"

"Certainly! From her in particular! The sight of her

free and easy grace alone delights me. I love my dog
very much, but in a different manner. I never beat my
dog, but I punish him sometimes in various ways, and
he understands every time that he is being punished.
He shows his repentance and begs forgiveness."

"How do you punish him if you don't beat him?"

"Very simply. I do not caress him. I talk to him
coldly and reproachfully. He grieves over it very much,
and begs until I am friendly again. Then he performs
a real joy dance. As far as the cat is concerned, I am
powerless."

"And this impotence pleases you?"

"Think what you will, Farmer. Yes, it does please me."

"Don't you go teaching the children such nonsense!"

"The children? I forbid them to incite dogs against
cats."

"That is all right. I agree with you there."

"It is really awful that one should always have to
defend cats! They are far nobler than dogs."

"Indeed! What next?"

"It's true! Far nobler than dogs. What is the dog's

kinship? Yes, you may produce as many breeds of dogs as you like, but try to breed cats—that is much more difficult, almost impossible. Cats are not suitable because they are too noble. Whom can the dog claim as relations? The wolf, the fox—that is almost all."

"Well, and is the cat's family anything to write home about?"

"Of course it is! She is of royal descent!"

"'Royal'? You're a fine democrat!"

"I am! As a man among men. But in nature, among free creatures, democracy is quite helpless. Think of the bull and the rabbit, the cock and the eagle, the deer and the weasel . . ."

"I am curious to hear about the royal associations of the cat!"

"With pleasure! The lion and the tiger, the kings of the animal world! I cannot see pussy walk, behold her elegant, graceful, brave gait, so effortless, springy and light, without thinking of the lion, the tiger and the panther, who have the very same attitude, the same commanding air. This association is forever present in my mind. It inspires me and gives me new vigor. It lends nobility to my humdrum existence, purifies the air I breathe . . ."

"It is impossible to talk to you, Teacher. You are too highly strung."

"I'm afraid you're right. We shall never see eye-to-eye."

"Thank heavens for that. I have no wish to see eye-to-eye with you!"

"I feel the same, thank heavens! So don't let us waste any more words. Good-bye!"

The farmer went away, muttering crossly.

"Ah!" the teacher breathed deeply, looked out into the dusky plain, listened to the melodious rustling of the trees, and then turned and entered his room. Djibi was fast asleep in a corner of the settee. Her sleep had the complete abandon, trust and carefreeness of an animal who is conscious of man's protection against all evils. Very softly the teacher stroked her silky fur and felt how thin her body still was. He was strangely touched by it.

Djibi woke up, looked round drowsily, saw the

teacher who was bending over her and began to purr loudly. The teacher smiled. "Will you feel at home with us, little puss?"

Djibi purred even louder, as if in reply.

"You shall have a good time," he continued. "You'll get sweet milk and anything else you are fond of."

Djibi had not changed her position. But now she turned slowly and languidly rolled on her back, with her legs in the air, and stretched comfortably.

"That's right, pussy! Enjoy yourself. You quite deserve it."

But as his caressing hand touched her injured thigh, where the bullet was still lodged, she winced and jumped up, whimpering—her wail seemed to accuse him.

"I see," he said, softly, "you want me to leave it until we are better acquainted. Now you shall have some more milk."

He got the jug, filled an earthenware saucer, and put it down on the floor. Djibi watched him attentively.

"Go on, pussy, drink," he coaxed.

Djibi jumped down on the floor, emitted a short purr, sat down in front of the saucer and drank.

"Now, my little one," whispered the teacher. "We shall be good friends. I'll do all I can to achieve this end."

Djibi did not allow herself to be disturbed.

She went on drinking.

The friendship was firmly established within a fortnight, and looked like growing stronger every day. Bertha, the teacher's wife, was also nice to Djibi.

The teacher was very pleased at the good relations.

He cared for Djibi's well-being, but left her to her own devices, and caressed her only when she purred to show her willingness.

He was pleased to see her catch mice, and equally pleased that she seemed to pay no attention to the chickens.

She has certainly lived among people, he thought. She knows exactly how to behave. What may have happened to her? Has she been ill-treated? Perhaps even driven away? Men are so heartless, especially with regard to cats.

Then happened the incident with the pigeon. The

teacher's pigeons were walking about among the chickens in the yard, unsuspecting, preening themselves coquettishly and cooing lovingly to each other.

On a previous occasion the teacher had observed Djibi lurking suspiciously in the vicinity of the peaceful birds.

He was now standing in his room looking into the yard through his window.

Djibi's lurking manner, the way in which she stalked up to the pigeons, suddenly revealed to him the beast of prey with terrifying clarity.

He rushed out as quickly as he could. But he came too late.

Djibi had already seized a pigeon which was weakly fluttering its wings.

Now the situation became critical.

On no account must he let her have her prey. But to snatch it away from her without further ado might jeopardize their young friendship.

He approached Djibi and talked to her coaxingly.

She remained sitting quietly and did not run away with the bleeding bird in her grasp. This he already regarded as a success.

Now he bent toward her, stroked her and gently tried to withdraw the dead bird.

It was not easy, because Djibi held it tightly in her teeth.

"Pussy," he said. "Pussy, be good. Give me the pigeon! Come, give it to me! You mustn't do it, it's nasty! My dear pussy will do no such thing. She is good, isn't she? She will leave the pigeons in peace!"

At last he held the dead pigeon in his hands.

He coaxed Djibi lovingly to compensate her for her loss. "There is no need for you to eat pigeons, is there, darling? You can have any tasty bits you like! You can catch mice, or even rats, but you must leave the pigeons alone! You will, won't you?"

He thought: "If I succeed in weaning her from this habit, I will have achieved a great deal. As it is, she checks her wild instincts. She does not touch the chickens. The pigeons . . . well, it is a relapse, it must not happen again."

He took a spade, dug a little hole in the ground and buried the pigeon. Djibi watched him closely all the time. When the pigeon had disappeared in the earth, she looked at him in great surprise.

"Yes, my dear," he said softly, "isn't it a pity to see the little thing go?"

With one graceful leap, Djibi sat on his shoulder, purring loudly and rubbing her head against his chin, and submitted to his caresses.

Does she want the pigeon back? he wondered. Or has she forgiven me for taking it away? He could not quite make her out, but continued to stroke her. Patience is needed, he thought. A great deal of patience.

In the coming weeks his patience was rewarded, because Djibi never touched the pigeons again; she passed them by as indifferently as the chickens.

· · ·

One day one of the schoolboys brought a canary, imprisoned in a tiny cage. "There, Teacher," he said. "Mother sent him for you, he can sing beautifully."

Now, a caged bird was just what the teacher did not like.

He would have liked to follow his first impulse and refuse the gift, but did not have the heart to offend the donor.

He thanked the boy, with a sigh, and immediately procured himself as large a cage as possible.

But how to protect the small singer from the cat?

At his wife's advice, he hung the new cage high up on the bare wall, filled the bowl with hemp seeds, put water in the beautiful bath, and let the bird, who until now had been fluttering forlornly in its narrow cage, into the new abode. He flew in with a touching gesture and a squeak of delight.

Mrs. Bertha christened him Hansi. She said: "Every canary is called Hansi."

At first Djibi took no notice of him at all.

As soon as Hansi got used to his new home, he began to warble softly. Then, growing bolder, he sang beautiful tunes, melodious airs. The room seemed to brighten up with his tireless singing.

The teacher listened spellbound and watched the bird's throat swell with the joyous effort of his song.

"I am glad you are feeling so happy up there, my little friend," he murmured.

"Look at the cat," warned Bertha.

Djibi seemed to listen to the song in surprise, apparently not realising whence the sound came. Then, attracted by the voice, she attempted a high jump, but slipped down the bare wall.

"Too short!" laughed the man.

"She'll soon hit the mark," observed Bertha. "At any rate, we must watch her."

But Djibi did not repeat her attempt; she stole away, as though ashamed at her failure.

The teacher followed her graceful retreat with amusement, and remembered the lions, of whom it is said that an unsuccessful attempt to seize their prey fills them with shame and causes them to slink away, abashed.

Hansi sang from dawn till dusk. Even later he would still chirp odd fragments of his song.

In the evening, the teacher climbed a ladder and covered the cage with a dark cloth, which he removed in the morning, as soon as the bird began to warble softly and shyly.

It was a homely, charming existence with this refreshing companion.

The teacher still retained his aversion against such confinement, but Hansi had won his entire affection, and he tried to persuade himself that this canary was a unique exception.

He was often deeply moved by the trust which Hansi showed him.

One day, about noon, the song broke off suddenly. The teacher, who was in the yard outside, heard Hansi fluttering.

He walked quietly into the room and stopped at the door.

He saw the cat crouching on the roof of the cage. After many vain attempts, she had succeeded in jumping up the bare wall.

Djibi's paws were pulling at the wire net which separated her from her victim. Hansi sat on the floor of the cage, faint with terror.

The teacher reflected.

There was no point in simply driving the cat away: she would only renew her attempt at the next opportunity.

He suddenly remembered the sling, with which he used to frighten birds of prey away from the poultry yard. It was lying in the kitchen cupboard.

He got it out quickly.

The cat must suspect nothing; she must not see him when she was hit.

He leaned against the doorpost and took an aim at her.

Djibi did not notice him in her eager chase of the

bird. A frightened wail escaped her: she was hit by the little stone.

Complaining, she escaped, saw the teacher, and ran up to him.

He received her tenderly. "What is it, pussy? Where does it hurt?"

"What a hypocrite I am!" he said to himself, but could not help grinning.

Djibi went round him with her tail in the air, rubbed against his legs and accepted his consolation.

"I hope this is the end of her attacks on Hansi," he thought.

Hansi did not sing any more that day. The teacher wanted to cheer him up and whistled all sorts of tunes. Usually the canary would join in quickly and heartily, but today he merely responded occasionally with a faint chirping. The shock had apparently shaken him badly.

On the following days the teacher kept Djibi under close observation.

But she paid no further attention to the cage. Her experience had cured her.

Very soon Hansi was singing merrily again. Djibi lay on her rug, asleep after her painstaking toilet.

Peace reigned in the house.

The storms of autumn raged, then it snowed. A fire crackled in the fireplace and warmed the living room. The kitchen range radiated glowing heat almost without cease.

Djibi had her favorite cozy places: in the living room by the fireplace and in the kitchen near the stove.

Her friendship with the teacher grew and deepened daily, and her relations with Tasso, the big Airedale, were also amicable.

The cold had driven Tasso into the house. He lay in front of the fire and stared into the flames.

No sooner had Djibi gotten friendly with Tasso than she began to tyrannize him.

When it was time to go to bed in the evening, she cuddled into Tasso's flanks. But during the night she kicked and wriggled until she had the rug to herself.

When he sat in front of the fire she immediately settled down between his front legs. If, growing sleepy, he wanted to rest his head on his paws, he was reminded by a resounding slap from Djibi to keep his head up, which he did good-naturedly.

The winter passed slowly.

The dog and the cat slept a great deal.

The teacher had no trouble with his pets.

When the spring's mild winds began to blow, tomcats started to call and pay their court to Djibi. They quarreled and howled until the early hours of the morning. Sometimes they indulged in the most violent and embittered fights.

Djibi was excited; she wanted to get out. The teacher had no intention of stopping her.

Her appearance increased the combatants' heat, and for several nights stormy scenes took place.

The tomcats fought passionately for the possession of the bride, while Djibi paraded among them with an innocent mien which increased their desires.

At last this period of warfare came to an end. Ruffled but obviously satisfied, Djibi returned home and subsided into almost continuous slumber.

After a few weeks her body began to swell. She was bearing her young.

Solicitously, the teacher saw that she had everything she needed and waited for the hour on which Djibi was to become a mother.

It took a little less than two months. He arranged for her a comfortable lying-in couch. "The princess may well be satisfied with the preparations," smiled Mrs. Bertha. There was a strained atmosphere in the house as Djibi's confinement approached.

She emitted murmuring, plaintive, tenderly purring sounds. Her expression was brave, longing and loving.

Tasso, considerate, kept away from her.

Three kittens appeared in quick succession.

Djibi's manner underwent a complete transformation.

She washed every baby kitten elaborately as soon as it was born, laid it down at her side and did not rest until the mite, still blind, found her breast.

She was touching in her gentle, tireless, and patient tenderness, though she herself was still in a state of complete exhaustion.

The glances which she threw at the teacher spoke of complete trust and peaceful rest.

She lay down sideways, with her little ones carefully placed at her nipples, watching them lovingly.

The teacher bent down to the mother and her children: "Well, pussy, you've done it! How do you feel now?"

She looked at him tenderly, and he ventured to stroke her. She began to purr softly and he said gaily: "Everything in order!"

"Of course it is!" nodded Mrs. Bertha, who was standing by. "A cat like her can stand a good deal more!"

Tasso approached, too, sniffing at Djibi and the kittens.

The teacher watched them anxiously. He feared an attack by the cat, who might resent the dog's intrusion and try to ward him off. But Djibi only raised her paw languidly and amicably slapped Tasso's snout.

He wagged his tail in excitement.

Hansi sang, chirped and warbled, full of enthusiasm.

A few days later, when the teacher was sitting contentedly in his armchair, Djibi came up to him, carrying a kitten in her mouth, jumped onto his lap and entrusted her child to him.

Then she brought the two remaining kittens, which she also left in his care, and finally joined them on his lap.

Tasso stood at the teacher's side and submitted to Djibi's playful slaps.

"Now you are all united!" said Bertha.

The young kittens developed rapidly. One was an image of the mother, the second had a yellow fur which accentuated her resemblance to a lioness, and the third had black stripes.

All three showed a childlike, fascinating gracefulness.

Djibi herself became a child again, so eagerly did she play with her young ones, fall in with their whims and their droll fancies.

The teacher was so enchanted by their sight that he neglected his own work.

For hours he sat with them, holding a ball of wool

by a loose thread, and watched the antics of the three kittens trying to catch it. When the mother joined in, in a solemn attempt to teach her youngsters, his delight knew no bounds.

The singing of the canary, whose cage was now hung far lower, and Tasso's sociable company, added to his high spirits.

One day the farmer called again:

"Good heavens, man, four cats!" He was positively alarmed.

"Well, what about it?"

"What are you going to do with four cats?"

"Nothing, Farmer, nothing! I'm enjoying myself with them."

"Will you never learn any sense?"

"Not in the way you define sense!"

"You mean you will keep all four cats?"

"Of course!"

"Of the three kittens, you should have at least drowned two!"

"*Should* have?"

"Naturally!"

"I am no murderer!"

"Don't talk such nonsense!"

"It is no nonsense. Such an action is, in my opinion, nothing but murder."

"What next! Drowning a couple of newborn kittens is no murder!"

"What is it, then?"

"Nothing! Absolutely nothing! If I shoot my dog, am I a murderer?"

"Certainly; from a higher point of view, you are a murderer."

"Leave me alone with your higher point of view. You are a fool."

"You're right, quite right. And because I am a fool, I am not a farmer, but a mere teacher. Nothing more."

"Even as a teacher you could have made your way and gotten on in the world. It only requires good management."

"What for? I don't care a jot for your so-called prosperity." The teacher snapped his fingers. "The children are fond of me; even you still like me quite well from your schooldays. Or don't you?"

"Of course I do. I like you very well!"

"There you are! My ambition is satisfied. I am quite content."

"But next year... what will happen? Won't you have eight or even ten cats roaming about the place?"

"Perhaps. It is not for me to say."

"Who but you can prevent it? In whose hands is it?"

The teacher shrugged his shoulders and grinned.

"It is entirely pussy's affair."

"But... that is..."

"That is only natural," interrupted the teacher.

"And you're going to raise every litter?"

"Look how they enjoy their existence!" He pointed at the gay dancing kittens.

"You'll come to a bad end!"

"Don't worry, farmer, the end comes to every one of us. Besides, the end is always bad, just because it is the end."

"Aren't you frightened of it?"

"No. I am not frightened of anything! A bad conscience would torment me out of my sleep at night, but I have no bad conscience. Therefore, I am not afraid of the end."

"Do you believe in God at all?"

"I believe in God. I worship him in every living being . . . that is more than you do."

"More than I? I deny it!"

"Understand me well! I worship God with every kindness I show to our dumb brothers. All living creatures are our dumb brothers, the children of the Great Creator. Remember, every good deed toward our dumb brothers is a prayer to God!"

"I'll say no more. You have even succeeded in reconciling the worst enemies!"

"What do you mean?"

The farmer pointed in surprise to Tasso, who was rolling one of the kittens, while Djibi looked happily on.

"Dog and cat," said the teacher, "are, of course, jealous of each other. That is quite true. But man has whipped this jealousy into hatred and strife, and man alone can make peace between them again."

"You are referring to yourself, aren't you?"

"Only because I cannot think of anybody else at the moment!"

"Because you are . . . you are an exception."

"Unfortunately, most unfortunately! I wish I weren't."

When it got warm, the teacher brought the three kittens with their mother out into the yard, to enjoy the sunshine and the fresh air. For the same reason he put the canary's cage on the windowsill.

A few days later an incident occurred which cost the life of the lion-colored kitten.

The summer heat cast a drowsy spell on animals and people alike.

Tasso was resting in the shade, Djibi slept at his side, and the teacher dozed on the couch in the cool room. One of the three kittens lay in the full sun, the other two in the shade by the fountain.

Hansi alone was lively, enjoying to the full the

glowing air, the smell of the fields, and the brightness of the day. He sang as loudly as he could, and his melodious voice was vigorous and jubilant.

Suddenly a terrier came tearing into the peaceful scene. He ran fast, as though possessed, and on his passage seized the yellow kitten by her neck, smashed her fragile spine and threw the dead body aside.

Only a faint, plaintive sound escaped the kitten as she met her death.

But this feeble tone was sufficient to alarm Djibi. She jumped to her feet. As soon as the terrier saw the cat he flew at her.

A well-aimed blow made him reel back. All this happened so quickly that Djibi barely had time to arch her back. She stood there, ready for the fight. The terrier returned to the attack. He whined painfully under Djibi's claws, retreated, but remained standing in front of his enemy, watchful.

In the meantime, Tasso had woken up; he put an end to the tension by throwing himself at the terrier, who at first turned a somersault and then escaped.

Suddenly Djibi discovered her dead child.

Without a moment's hesitation she chased the fugitive, overtook him, jumped on his back and belabored him mercilessly with furious blows until he was streaming with blood.

He howled loudly, frantic with terror and pain.

He had no alternative but to roll on the floor, and thus rid himself of the raving cat. He took advantage of it to escape with the utmost haste from the scene of his misdeed.

Tasso followed him and barked so violently that the terrier redoubled his speed.

The row had drawn the teacher to his door. He quickly reached for Djibi and lifted her, though she resisted.

For a long time he tried to calm her agitation, and partly succeeded when he picked up the two little kittens and showed them to her. She received the youngsters tenderly, sniffed at them and listened attentively to their low purring. Finally there was a proper trio, with a loud purring overtone and two thin accompaniments. The teacher listened, delighted, and thought the crisis was over.

But Djibi was pulling to get down from his arms to the spot where the body of the kitten lay. She found no peace, escaped the teacher's caresses, jumped down to the ground with a faint wail and crouched by the side of her dead child, mourning her with touching laments.

The teacher did his best to coax her away. He succeeded only after a long while.

Then he fetched the dead kitten and buried it secretly.

Some weeks later a change came over the teacher.

He saw that Djibi neglected her young and that they all began to grow strangers to each other.

Mrs. Bertha, who was by no means unfriendly, but who had no sentimental attitude to animals, once jokingly called her husband "a wet rag."

At first these words seemed to make no impression on him. But as time went on, he noticed they stuck to him, that they rankled in his heart, and stirred his whole being into revolt.

A wet rag!

He searched his soul, gave himself a candid account of his behavior, and found that Bertha was right.

The fact that he resented this description, that the cap seemed to fit, was in itself sufficient proof that Bertha's assertion was well-founded.

But he did not want to be a wet rag; he determined to be harsher, yes, to grow hard.

When reflecting in this manner, he remembered many of the farmer's arguments which now seemed convincing to him. He adopted the farmer's viewpoint almost entirely, including the reproaches directed against himself. His emotional arguments, by which he had stood with such determination, now melted away. His former opinions were shattered like a fragile piece of china.

He was a failure in his own eyes!

Everyone had been treating him with condescending tolerance, as a sentimental ass . . .

Sentimental . . . exaggerating . . . in short, a fool!

He did not realize that he was now going too far in the opposite direction.

He went about cold and stiff, took only a mild pleasure in the canary's joyous song, and pretended to be hard. No longer a wet rag!

Djibi sensed the coldness in the attitude of her two-legged friend. She could, of course, not guess that this restraint was self-imposed, like a mask, beneath which lay hidden the kind, familiar, and well-loved face. Djibi did not possess so much subtle penetration.

But she felt neglected. True to her character, she was ready to retaliate, and on her part ignored the teacher.

Bertha noticed it very soon and declared: "Now she is proving what I have always maintained: cats know no attachment."

The teacher shrugged his shoulders as though such things were of no consequence to him. Internally, however, he grieved over Djibi's conduct. He longed to re-establish the old familiarity, to take Djibi in his arms and press her to his heart, so that she might put her head under his chin and purr as she used to do in the past.

But he restrained himself sternly.

In the meantime, Djibi was squatting outside with apparent unconcern, surrounded by three tomcats who wooed her with atrocious, ear-splitting howls. Soon they were no longer content with their concert, but fell furiously over each other, growing more violent and ferocious every minute. Djibi looked on with complete calm and obvious enjoyment.

Hissing, spluttering, growling, yells of fury, cries of pain.

At last the teacher's wife put an end to the performance. She emptied a pail of water out of the window and shouted to Tasso: "Get the cats!" at which she was shocked herself.

An exclamation of protest escaped the teacher.

"Really, Bertha!"

The tomcats fled in all directions.

Djibi sought refuge in the room.

Tasso wagged his stump a little, and it seemed as though he were smiling.

This little incident stabbed the teacher's heart, but he did violence to himself and remained silent. He went to the birdcage and whispered: "Hansi . . ."

"Peep!" said the canary, turning his head; he repeated "Peep" and began to warble his song.

Mrs. Bertha said, with a smile: "I like him best of all your menagerie. At least he can sing, and he gives no trouble!"

Since Djibi felt neglected in the house, she began to stray.

At first only for part of the day; then she disappeared for days on end and nobody knew where she had got to.

She sat in the fields, preying on mice; nor did she disdain grasshoppers and frogs.

The teacher often used to stand outside and call: "Pussy! Pussy!"

"Leave her, for goodness' sake!" said Bertha. "She'll turn up when she wants her food or milk."

It was no small effort to the teacher to suppress his attachment to Djibi.

The way Bertha spoke and acted, her attitude to animals and even to himself gradually seemed to him too dry and matter of fact, sometimes still worse—just unfeeling.

He grew internally estranged from his wife.

This made him very unhappy, because, without Bertha, yes, and without Djibi, too, he felt very lonely.

He had picked Djibi up in the street. She had come toward him trustingly, in search of protection. The confidence of this graceful creature had filled him with joy. Bertha, too, seemed fond of Djibi at the beginning.

What had happened to change everything so? He could not understand it, and his state of mind did not improve.

He just had a tender disposition.

A "wet rag"!

Well, yes, so what of it?

He had been happy.

Why try to change himself?

One man is a bristling brush, the other a wet rag. That is how things are in life.

Some people move between these two extremes, and have no conflicts or internal battles, but they are uninteresting as a result.

In any event the position was that the teacher was anxious to know everything about Djibi, but knew nothing. He was more annoyed with her than he was willing to admit. After all, he was responsible for her.

Of course, he still had Tasso and the canary; but he felt certain of these two and they meant less to him.

As usual, those who are dependable get least praise and attention.

One evening Tasso came running home, carrying Djibi in his mouth. She seemed limp and lifeless.

The teacher was speechless with alarm. He thought Tasso had killed Djibi. Mrs. Bertha seemed to have come to a similar conclusion, for she gave a shocked exclamation.

But Tasso put Djibi down on the floor, and she began rubbing herself against him, her tail in the air.

Only the two of them, the dog and the cat, knew that Tasso had rescued her, as he had done many times before.

He had delivered her from a boy who liked to torture animals but feared big dogs.

This boy, whose name was William, was the son of a locksmith, twelve years old, stocky, sullen, with brown hair which grew nearly down to his eyes, leaving hardly any forehead. Once before he had stolen up to the teacher's yard, where he tried to catch Djibi and tie a tin to her tail.

Tasso's growling and Djibi's frightened shrieks had attracted Bertha's attention and she ran out, surprised William, caught him by his shock of hair, shook him vigorously and gave him a smacking slap on the face.

"What is going on here?" asked the teacher, coming out of the house. "What are you doing here, William?"

The boy stood there with a lowered head and a stubborn expression.

"Oh, he is a nasty fellow!" said Mrs. Bertha, furious. "A miserable tormentor of animals! He got what he deserved!" She boxed his ears again, and his face turned purple.

"Are you a tormentor of animals?" said the teacher, softly. "Come here for a minute."

William did not move, persisted in his stubborn silence, remained inaccessible.

"Well, I shall have to go to you," smiled the teacher. He walked up to the boy, put his hand on his shoulder and, although William remained motionless, he immediately felt the boy's violent resistance to this gentle touch.

"Why do you torture animals?"

No reply.

"Does it give you pleasure?"

No reply.

"Look, William, to us human beings animals are dumb. They have a language of their own, but we are unable to understand it—certainly very little of what they wish to express. Are you listening?"

William stared at the ground and was silent.

"Of course you're listening," continued the teacher.

"We are often puzzled by the dumb creatures, but they are helpless, defenseless, and entirely in our power."

Silence.

"Well, my dear, is it right to abuse this power? No, a hundred times no! It is horrid!"

William did not raise his eyes from the ground.

"When such a tortured animal cries out in pain, aren't you ashamed of yourself?"

The teacher felt that the vicious boy was silently jeering at him, but he still kept his temper.

"Some of your victims have no voices at all. The lizard you torture, the beetles whose wings you tear off, the crickets and grasshoppers whom you ill-treat . . . Do you realize what a powerful indictment is growing against you? Do you know how your evil deeds befoul God's earth?"

The boy refused to come out of his stubborn silence.

"Animals flee from you," continued the teacher. "But people, too, avoid you; they, too, notice that you are an enemy, a cruel, cowardly fellow. You will win nobody's love; if you don't change, you'll be a marked man!"

William raised his eyes for a moment and threw the teacher a glance full of hatred.

"Go!" said the teacher, with unusual vehemence. "Go, and don't come near this place again!"

William turned and walked slowly out of the yard, without a word.

One day, Djibi returned home from the fields, or so the teacher thought.

She no longer had her usual amiable expression; she seemed to be conscious of having committed some misdeed.

She ignored the teacher and barely touched the milk Bertha put before her.

When the teacher tried to coax her into a better mood she didn't take any notice of him. Her behavior was strange, almost hostile.

Mrs. Bertha shook her head: "There is something wrong with the cat."

Toward the evening, Djibi took the first opportunity to escape out of doors. Outside, a huge Persian tomcat was waiting for her. Quietly huddled into herself, she sat opposite him.

The Persian started the most atrocious catcalls, screeching and howling. Bertha wanted to chase him away with a pail of water.

"Don't," begged the teacher, "don't! He is wooing pussy."

"I can't stand it any longer," said Bertha.

"I am not very fond of this concert myself," replied the teacher, "but we have to bear it."

"Why do we have to?" asked his wife.

"Because it is the love play of the cats, and we must not disturb the animals in their lovemaking."

"But I can't bear it!" cried Bertha. "This horrible noise gets on my nerves."

"Stuff your ears with cotton wool," joked the teacher.

Bertha got cross. "You wet rag!"

"You have already intimidated me once with this word," said the teacher. "I took it to heart then, and got estranged from pussy. Now I have resigned myself to being a wet rag."

"A fine state of affairs!" exclaimed Bertha.

"It certainly is." The teacher spoke with emphasis. "I can only be happy if there is harmony between the animals and me."

"And you place no value on being at harmony with me?"

"Oh, Bertha!" The teacher took her hand. "We two are human beings, man and wife; we can talk to each other. That is decisive. We shall always understand each other."

All this time the tomcat was growling, hissing, screeching outside.

"Of course we shall understand each other." Bertha now spoke very softly, quickly seized the pail and threw the water out of the window. She sighed with relief as the tomcat fled and Djibi crept indoors.

Djibi shook off the water from her fur and huddled into a corner of the settee. The teacher went up to her, stroked her and spoke very gently:

"Pussy, dear, beautiful pussy, what is the matter with you?"

Djibi tolerated his caresses, but did not respond.

As the teacher continued to stroke her and talk to her entreatingly, Bertha said impatiently: "Don't always make such a fuss of her!"

Djibi escaped and hurried out of the room.

He went to the door and called: "Pussy, pussy!"

But Djibi was nowhere to be seen.

Sadly, he returned. "Now you have chased her away," he said to his wife.

"I have done her no harm," protested Bertha. "She has gone to look for her lover."

The farmer called again.

"Teacher, I've acquired something new!"

"What is it?"

"Guess!"

"Pigs?"

"I had gotten those long ago!"

"Turkeys?"

"Wrong again!"

"I don't really know."

"Something that breeds quickly, needs little attention, and tastes as good as chicken."

"Rabbits?"

"You've got it! Rabbits. Twenty of them. I got them cheaply off a dealer. We have already eaten several. Delicious, I tell you! And yet their number has not diminished. You ought to get yourself some!"

"What for?"

"For eating, of course!"

"No. If I keep rabbits, I get friendly with them, and I don't like eating personal acquaintances."

"But, Teacher, you eat veal and pork."

"Of course, but I have never seen the calves and pigs."

"I don't think you are being consistent."

"Life is full of inconsistencies, my dear chap!"

"You're making things difficult for yourself, aren't you?"

"I don't think we live to make things easy for ourselves."

"On the contrary, in my opinion, one should try and make things as easy as possible."

"Perhaps you're right. But it's not in my temperament."

Mrs. Bertha intervened in the conversation.

"No, Farmer, my husband likes things to be difficult! He believes it is best so."

"Well," said the farmer to her, "I don't envy you!"

When he had left, the teacher asked his wife: "Would you like to kill rabbits and eat them?"

Bertha shuddered and shook her head. "How can you say such a thing?"

Modest, trusting, shy, and yet proud, a lovely Angora cat came one day into the teacher's house.

Dazzlingly white, with long hair, she immediately won the affection of the teacher and his wife.

In the beginning she only appeared for a short while and vanished again when Djibi came home.

But as Djibi seemed to pay her no attention, Snowwhite used to stay longer, thereby indicating that she began to feel at home.

"Where does she come from?" wondered the teacher.

"Nobody in the whole village has such a magnificent creature."

"You know what cats are," replied Bertha, "and you also know the incredible brutality of most people. She has certainly been ill-treated somewhere, or sadly neglected."

"She is beautiful!" said the teacher.

"Lovely!" agreed Bertha. "Come here, you beauty."

To the surprise of both the teacher and his wife, the Angora cat jumped gracefully into Bertha's lap. Bertha put her arms round her, and the cat cuddled snugly into her bosom, swinging her tail to and fro.

"For once her choice has fallen on me!" laughed Bertha.

"But she doesn't purr," said the teacher.

Bertha stroked the cat. "As smooth and soft as silk," she declared appreciatively. "Call her! Perhaps she'll go to you, too."

The teacher was standing a few paces away.

"Pussy! Beautiful pussy!" he coaxed softly.

The Angora cat pricked her ears, and lifted her head slowly. Her large, yellow eyes, with their narrow, dark pupils, looked searchingly round the room: her mien had a thoughtful expression, as though she were considering something.

Then she flew to his shoulder in one single leap.

He wanted to touch her, but she slid past his face to his other shoulder and returned again, brushing his chin. He could hear and feel her sharp claws digging into his coat.

Now she sat crouching on his shoulder, her shimmering body pressed against his throat and cheek, vigorously tapping his back with her tail.

Suddenly the room resounded with a gay, loud purring, so bright and winning that both people burst out laughing. The laughter increased the Angora cat's good humor; she purred still louder in high-pitched tones, and it was almost as if she were singing a particularly jolly song.

The canary took it as an invitation and began to warble.

The Angora cat paid no heed to the singer. She slipped down to the floor, marched about the room, with an air of inspecting her new home.

Composedly, she peered into every corner, inspected every seat. She even majestically passed by the saucer of milk which Bertha put down for her. She appeared to be guided solely by her own resolve, and nothing seemed to disconcert her.

Tasso came in, wagging his tail in a friendly fashion.

"This is a dangerous test," whispered the teacher anxiously.

But the Angora cat did not arch her back; she ran to the dog's encounter, raised herself and embraced his neck. He sniffed at her with puffing breath.

"Now she'll hit out," said the teacher, ready to intervene.

However, no attack followed.

The cat and the dog looked into each other's eyes. The Angora cat purred, and Tasso licked her face.

Now the cat turned away from him to her milk saucer and drank a little.

Tasso stood looking on, and his attitude seemed to encourage the guest to enjoy her meal.

Suddenly the Angora cat pricked her ears and turned her head to the window, listening.

True enough, Djibi jumped in through the window.

She had hardly seen the Angora cat before she threw herself at her, hissing furiously.

Neither the teacher nor his wife were able to say how it happened.

The Angora cat had not raised a paw, but she nevertheless thrust Djibi violently against the wall. The latter lay there in a heap, whimpering pitifully.

The teacher picked her up tenderly. "No, I won't allow this noble lady to ill-treat you! You are my good old pussy, aren't you?"

Djibi did not purr, nor did she rub her head against the teacher's chin. She lay quietly in his arms as he caressed her, and from time to time emitted a low moan.

The teacher turned to his wife. "Do you think she is all right? Perhaps the new cat has injured her . . ."

"Don't worry," reassured his wife. "You know how

tough cats are. The blow she has received is hardly worth mentioning!"

The teacher tickled Djibi fondly. "What is wrong with you, then, puss?"

"Nothing is wrong with her!" exclaimed Bertha. "She is simply offended, and jealous!"

"Come, puss, be good again! You really have no reason to be jealous. True, the white lady is prettier and stronger than you are, but she shall not hurt you anymore. You are and remain my darling!"

But Djibi would not be consoled or reconciled. The teacher kept her in his arms for a long time, but could not induce her to show any of her usual friendly gestures. After a time he noticed that Djibi pulled away from him.

He would not admit it at first, but finally had to give in.

Djibi slipped down to the floor.

It struck him that on this occasion she did not parade proudly around his legs with her tail high, but simply ran away, indifferent. At the first opportunity she slipped out through the door.

From now on the Angora cat reigned supreme in the teacher's house. There were neither quarrels nor fights between her and Djibi. The two cats even drank their milk cordially out of the same saucer.

Djibi slept with Tasso, as before, and still domineered him.

The Angora cat, superior, slept alone in a corner of the couch.

She did not make a single attack on the canary; in the yard she walked among the chickens and the pigeons without even deigning to bestow a look upon them.

Her behavior to Tasso was extremely courteous, and she did not attempt to subjugate him. One might describe their attitude to each other as one of friendly respect.

But Tasso's unshakable love belonged to Djibi; and this, as well as his constant protection, helped Djibi to bear the presence of the Angora cat. She was clearly relying on Tasso's support in the event of a clash with the intruder.

Tasso also assisted her in her secret expeditions

against the farmer's rabbits. He never touched a rabbit himself, but carefully guarded Djibi while she seized her prey. He always felt the approach of danger, quickly caught Djibi in his teeth and carried her home.

Djibi never resisted him in the slightest. She submitted to his decisions without any opposition; apparently it never occurred to her to question his judgement in such cases, though she domineered him in every other respect. She appeared to understand that he was her protector.

Bertha was very pleased with the Angora cat. She said to her husband: "She is a charming companion, like the canary. They both give no trouble."

He agreed: "Yes, the bird delights us with his song, and the white lady with her beauty."

"And her nobility," added Bertha.

They had no idea of Djibi's doings, nor of her secret complicity with Tasso.

Their suspicions were first aroused when the farmer called one day, in great agitation.

"Some beast is stealing my rabbits!" he cried. "A rabbit

every day!" The farmer banged his fist on the table.

"Perhaps a fox," said Bertha.

"Or a marten," suggested the teacher.

"A marten, a marten!" the farmer sneered, with an angry laugh. "You ought to know better! A marten would have killed all the rabbits in one go!"

"Why don't you secure your rabbit hutch so that no one can get at it, neither fox nor marten?" asked Bertha.

"A fox!" grunted the farmer. "Have you ever heard of a fox, who would come and take a rabbit every night?"

"Hardly likely," admitted the teacher.

"It's a clever beast!" reflected the farmer.

"At any rate, cleverer than you are," mocked Bertha.

"If I get hold of the brute, I'll kill it on the spot!" threatened the farmer.

Djibi squeezed anxiously past him and ran out, followed by Tasso, who growled as he passed the farmer.

"Why does the dog growl at you?" The teacher glanced suspiciously at the farmer. "It isn't like him!"

The farmer shrugged his shoulders. "No idea! I've never done anything to Tasso."

"How queer," said the teacher in a strange voice.

"Ah, who is this?" exclaimed the farmer, as though he had only just noticed the Angora cat lying in the corner of the settee. It was obvious that he was playacting in order to change the subject of the conversation. "She is a beauty! Even I would not have minded such a cat! How long has she been with you?"

The teacher was silent.

Bertha supplied the information: "A few days."

"Where did you get her from?" asked the farmer.

"She came by herself," replied Bertha.

The farmer was now bending over the Angora cat, who took no notice of him. "Why didn't you come to me? I would have been very pleased!"

Bertha laughed: "How was she to know it? You detest cats!"

"But such a gorgeous specimen . . ." Clumsily his hand went over her back. "What a fur! One could really fall in love with her!"

The cat looked at him with an air of dignified

surprise. Her attitude said clearly: "I don't know you! You don't know me! No familiarities, please!"

She got up, indicating her displeasure, and moved to another corner of the settee.

The farmer turned away, offended. "What an uppish creature! It's not my loss if she won't have me as a friend."

"One must have the gift to be a friend," smiled the teacher. "Animals feel it at once. You have little aptitude for friendship."

"I! Little aptitude for friendship! But I have been your friend for a long time!"

"You're a pleasant neighbor, but not really what I would call a friend."

"In this case, you're not a true friend to me, either."

"It's different in my case. You were my pupil for a long time! You remember that I was always a friend of my pupils, don't you?"

"Yes, but now I'm no longer your pupil. Times change . . ."

"Perhaps, but they don't change me! Weren't you always able to speak your mind to me?"

"That's true enough."

"Was I ever angry when you contradicted me? And you did so often enough!"

"Look at Snowwhite!" interrupted Bertha. "Does she want to go to you?"

"Beautiful Snowwhite," called the teacher. "Come, please come!"

The Angora cat had pulled herself up, and leaped toward him, landing rather painfully on his stomach.

The teacher helped her to climb up to his shoulder. "Come on! Your claws are sharp enough!"

But the cat remained suspended on his chest, wagging her bushy tail. Then she suddenly jumped up to the teacher's neck, and, nestling against his cheek, started her melodious purring.

"I think I'd better go now, or I might become jealous!" said the farmer, with a forced smile.

Bertha's eyes twinkled as he went. "He is annoyed, and jealous in earnest!"

· · ·

Dusk was falling.

Glancing around him, the teacher said: "Pussy is out again!"

"What's surprising, about it?" retorted Bertha. "She is like all cats, and sneaks out at night for prey or love."

"Often for both," agreed the teacher.

"Anyhow, Tasso is with her, so you may be quite at ease."

"I'm not worried," the teacher assured her, "but the white lady never seems to show any desire to prowl at night."

"Yes, she is an exception," said Bertha praisingly.

At that moment—the teacher was just covering Hansi's cage for the night—they could hear Tasso's sudden howl of pain, as though under a blow.

The teacher started. "What was that?"

Bertha, also frightened, stammered: "It seemed to come from the farmer's place!"

So it did.

The farmer, while standing guard over his rabbits,

had caught Djibi in the act of killing one of them. He fell furiously over her and hit her cruelly, until she lost consciousness. When Tasso came to Djibi's rescue he received a violent and vicious kick.

All this happened in the course of a few seconds.

Before the teacher and his wife realized the full implication of what they had heard, Tasso appeared in a state of obvious intimidation, carrying the bleeding cat in his mouth, and laid her cautiously in front of the teacher, his eyes full of sadness.

Djibi was a pitiful and horrible sight. Her chest seemed battered in. Her nose and mouth were streaming with blood. Her eyes were shut. She was weakly gasping for breath.

She appeared to be dying.

"Pussy, my dear pussy," called the teacher, bending low over her, but not daring to touch her.

Mrs. Bertha, moved but helpful, applied a cold compress, which revived Djibi a little.

"Who could have reduced you to such a state?" The teacher was completely at a loss.

At that moment the farmer stormed in. He was triumphant.

"At last I've laid my hands on the rabbit thieves! Your cat, my dear fellow, and your fine dog! But they know better now!"

"Indeed!" said the teacher.

The farmer was unabashed. "Yes!" he replied grandly. "They'll remember me, and their punishment!"

"You call that a punishment?" The teacher's voice was cold and stony. "And what right have you to punish?"

The farmer began to shout: "And what right have these beasts to eat my rabbits?"

The teacher stared at him, motionless, without answering.

"You have nothing to say now, have you?"

Bertha pulled the farmer's sleeve. "Get away, quickly," she whispered to him. "When he flies into a temper, he rages like the devil."

"I'm not afraid!" bragged the farmer. "I'm in my right!"

"So, you're in your right!" The teacher spoke very softly as he approached the farmer. "We shall see about that!"

The farmer had no time to avoid the blow which sent him reeling back.

"Why didn't you sue me for damages?"

The farmer stood there, wide-eyed and open-mouthed. "Damages?"

"Yes! You would have been in your right then! But only then!" The teacher was calmer now.

"But would you have paid?" stammered the farmer.

"I am telling you what your rights are," repeated the teacher. "I always obey the law. But you have behaved like an enemy!"

"No! No!" protested the farmer. "I'm not your enemy!"

"No! And yet, look how you have ill-treated the poor creature! Dare you maintain that you are not an enemy?"

The farmer bent over Djibi, remaining silent for a while. Then he whispered: "I've had my deserved punishment. Forgive me! ..."

"I'll forgive you when the cat is able to walk across the room again. Not a minute sooner!"

The farmer turned to Bertha. "Help her! Make her well again!"

"I can't do miracles," she replied curtly.

The farmer lingered dejectedly for a few minutes, as though waiting for something. But the teacher ignored him, and he crept meekly out of the door.

Mrs. Bertha prepared a comfortable resting place for Djibi, a real convalescent bed, on the top of the chest. Then she gave the cat a few drops of brandy, which restored some of her strength.

The cold water applications also did her a great deal of good; they reduced the swellings, which went down slowly.

A few drops of brandy from time to time were very effective in reviving Djibi's spirits. Milk had to be forced upon her.

One day, when Djibi raised her little head to drink by herself, the battle against death was won.

The teacher hardly moved from her side, fondled and stroked her gently. At first Djibi made no response to these caresses.

The farmer inquired daily after Djibi's condition.

For a time Bertha had to reply: "No change!"

Then she could say: "A little better!"

This answer gave the farmer courage: he could beg for forgiveness.

"That's a great step forward!" said Bertha one day, as Djibi tried to get up and escape on hearing the farmer's voice. "A great step forward!" she repeated, while the farmer scratched his head and sighed: "Oh, Lord!"

The Angora cat began to welcome his advances now.

One day she even leaped at his chest, which at first gave him a considerable shock. Then he ventured to stroke her, clumsily, while she sat on his shoulder.

Her soft purring delighted him.

He did not move, but only whispered softly: "That's nice! That's lovely!"

At last, he summoned up sufficient courage to approach the teacher: "Don't be angry with me any longer!"

But the teacher turned his back on him.

The farmer asked, bewildered: "Will things never be the same between us again?"

Bertha consoled him: "When pussy can walk across the room . . . You know what my husband said . . . He is always true to his word. Have patience, it will not be long now."

"Does the teacher live here?" an elegant lady inquired at the door one day.

Before anyone had time to answer, the Angora cat, purring, leaped off the settee and out through the window at the sound of the voice.

"There you are, Mira! I thought so!" exclaimed the lady.

Mira paraded to and fro in front of the lady, traced large circles with her bushy tail, and her purring sounded again almost like a song.

"I am Mrs. Lauber. My husband is a solicitor in town. You have, no doubt, heard of him."

"No." The teacher made a gesture of regret. "We don't have the honor."

"But I know you," said the lady vivaciously. "At least, I know you by repute."

The teacher bowed slightly but remained silent. Mrs. Bertha said nothing either.

The lady continued: "That's why I came straight to you. I knew I would find Mira here!"

"Do you want to take the cat back?" asked Bertha.

The lady laughed: "It isn't as simple as all that!" She stepped into the room, followed by Mira, and continued gaily: "Take her away? You can hardly be serious! People like you are certainly aware of the fact that we don't own the animals, but are really owned by them."

"Quite true," nodded the teacher.

Mrs. Lauber carried on: "Actually we depend on the animals and are entirely at the mercy of their whims."

"But those who understand animals know they have no whims," said the teacher.

In the meantime, the Angora cat climbed up and down the settee, tracing large circles with her tail, but said nothing...

Mrs. Lauber turned to Mira and addressed her at some length: "When did I hurt your feelings, Mira? Was it my fault that we had to go away for my health, on doctor's orders? Couldn't you wait for our return? Did the cook ill-treat you, or anyone else? Believe me, I'm innocent. You shouldn't have run away. Anyhow, you're an intelligent creature, you know what is good for you!"

She turned round and smiled at the teacher and his wife. "As though she had sensed that this was the best place she could choose! Did she give you a lot of trouble?"

"Oh, not at all," Bertha assured her eagerly. "We are very fond of her."

"We shall find it hard to part from her," murmured the teacher.

Ms. Lauber went up to the settee, took Mira in her arms and said, "Come, Mira, we two belong together, don't we?"

But Mira was of a different opinion. She slipped away from the lady, back to the settee.

The teacher approached her: "Go, Mira," he said softly. "Go back nicely with your mistress."

As he spoke, Mira jumped onto his shoulder, pressed herself against his neck and cheek and broke into her loud, melodious purring. The teacher stood there, embarrassed: "What shall I do?" He was a comic sight in his confusion at the advances of the purring cat. Mrs. Lauber could not help laughing. But she immediately grew serious again. "Mira has expressed her opinion very clearly," she said, "though unfortunately not in my favor. Clever Mira! She does not wish to be disappointed by me a second time. Isn't the independence of her mind delightful?"

The teacher nodded, smiling, and stroked the Angora cat's fur.

"I could almost be angry with Mira for showing me so little attachment," continued Mrs. Lauber, "but that would be mean of me. How about it? Do you want to keep Mira?"

Mrs. Bertha, who had been watching the scene anxiously, beamed.

"Are you serious?"

"Certainly," Mrs. Lauber assured him. "I respect Mira's decision."

"In that case . . . Oh, in that case . . . ," stammered the teacher, "I thank you!"

"On the contrary, it's for me to thank you." Mrs. Lauber threw Mira a last glance, turned quickly away, murmured a farewell greeting and hurried out of the room.

"Poor lady," said the teacher. "The parting was hard for her."

So Mira stayed of her own free will, and the teacher and his wife could keep her with an easy conscience.

After a while, however, Mira became moody and quite unpredictable. She could be extremely friendly one minute, and really vicious the next.

Tasso suffered most from her changing moods. When he came into the kitchen, Mira adopted the hostile attitude of a cat used to expecting attacks from strange dogs, arched her back and spat wildly.

Tasso was taken aback, but still thought it was only a game.

But when sharp claws dug deep into his bleeding snout, he growled and tried to seize Mira.

"Mira," intervened the teacher. "How can you plague your good comrade so?"

Mira pressed herself coyly against the teacher's caressing hands.

He smiled: "So you're friends again!"

But Mira still persisted in her aggressiveness.

This happened day after day.

At last the peaceable, gentle dog lost his patience.

When Mira had scratched his face again one day, he caught her in his powerful jaws, swung the screaming cat in the air, shook her violently and threw her down on the floor.

Mira's fur was tousled, but she was unhurt. She remained stretched out, pretending to be unconscious.

"What is the matter with you two?" called the teacher who had come in on hearing the cat scream.

Tasso wagged his tail eagerly, showing his readiness
for peace.

"Leave them alone!" said Bertha. "They're only playing."

"No," replied the teacher. "That is not a game. The
dog is bleeding."

It was, indeed, not a game, but earnest warfare.

Quick as lightning, Mira leap to her feet, trying to
jump at Tasso's neck.

But the embittered dog caught her by the breast, and
this time really bit her. She sank to the floor, streaming
with blood.

"Tasso!" cried the teacher. "Tasso!"

But Tasso paid no heed.

Growling, he searched for his enemy's throat, found
it, and bit again.

The cat's deep groans and her death rattle were
clearly audible.

The teacher tried to pull the dog away, but in vain.

"He is killing her!" cried Bertha, appalled.

Tasso, the good Tasso, was no longer meek and
gentle; he really killed the treacherous Mira.

In his rage he was insensible to the teacher's shaking and pulling; his fangs held on to Mira's snow-white breast, which was now red with blood, and he only let go of the cat when she was in a coma, though still breathing feebly.

He stood over her, watchful of her slightest movement, ready to pounce upon her again at a moment's notice.

But before long Mira had given up her last breath.

The teacher wrung his hands in despair. "That such a thing should happen in my house! That a dog like Tasso should commit such a foul murder!"

Bertha defended the dog. "You mustn't forget that he has been sorely tried."

"I can't understand it!" cried the teacher indignantly. "Before my own eyes! He did it in spite of my intervention! It is awful! My gentle Tasso!"

Tasso was lying on the floor, still and sad; at the sound of his name he pricked his ears.

"The gentlest dog can go wild at times," said the wife.

"He always used to be so patient," complained the teacher.

"The best patience comes to an end," excused Bertha.

She took the dead cat and carried her out.

"She was so superbly beautiful," mourned the teacher, when his wife returned.

"What is the use of beauty?" said Bertha earnestly. "If a creature is false, it is bound to come to a bad end."

"All the trouble I have taken with animals, all the affection I have bestowed upon them, has it all been in vain?" sighed the teacher.

At that moment Tasso laid his paw on the teacher's arm and looked up into his face.

"It is good of you to apologize, my dear fellow," said the teacher. "Perhaps it shows that peaceful cohabitation is still possible . . ."

Tasso did not cease to paw his master's arm.

"What more do you want of me?" the teacher glanced at the dog. His faithful look disarmed him immediately. He could not resist it.

"Yes, my Tasso," he said softly. "We are and remain friends . . . in spite of everything!"

But Tasso was longing for his master's stroking hand.

When the teacher caressed his head, Tasso emitted a sound which was in the nature of a jubilant sob.
Exultant with joy, he whirled madly about the room.
Although the teacher stood with his legs squarely
planted on the floor, the big dog nearly threw him over
as he affectionately jumped up to embrace him.

"Everything is all right again, Tasso!"

The teacher became gay again.

"Now we shall celebrate our reconciliation!"

"He has deserved it, the good fellow," said Bertha,
who was kneeling at Djibi's side. "Steady, there!" she
laughed as Tasso raced past her, nearly pushing her over
the sick cat.

The farmer put his head through the door and
asked: "How are things?"

"Looking up! Looking up all the time!" replied Bertha
happily.

He turned anxiously to the teacher. "Well, and you,
are you still angry with me?"

The teacher did not answer and looked away.

"Upon my word, you have no idea how sorry I am

for what happened!" pleaded the farmer. "You might say a kind word to me at last!"

The teacher remained silent.

"Heavens!" the farmer scratched his head. "If I had been a beast, you would have made it up with me long ago."

"Don't talk nonsense, man!" said Bertha kindly. "You're a human being, and that makes all the difference. You're not innocent, and you are responsible for your actions."

Tasso growled menacingly at the farmer.

"Have I nothing but enemies here?" complained the farmer.

"Don't be foolish!" reproached Bertha. "Nobody is your enemy here!"

"What about this dog? Does he growl at me because he likes me?"

"Oh, well, he never forgets anything," replied Bertha. "An animal never forgets a kindness, and certainly never a cruelty!"

"Come here, Tasso!" coaxed the farmer. "Come, my

good fellow, I shall do you no harm, none whatever!"

He stretched out his hand to stroke the dog, but Tasso snapped at him as though ready to bite, and edged away from him.

The farmer shook his head and said: "I'm sure that if the teacher talked to me, the dog would no longer be angry with me either."

"You know what condition my husband made," reminded Bertha. "Wait till the cat can walk across the room."

"Will she be able to do it?"

"I hope so," smiled Bertha. "I even hope it will not be long now."

"Will she recover fully?" The farmer stepped nearer.

Before Bertha could reply, Djibi gathered herself up with a violent hiss and tried to run away.

"She has given you her answer in person," said Bertha, holding Djibi down.

The farmer murmured sadly: "I could hit myself!"

"It seems to me my husband has seen to that!"

The farmer struggled with his embarrassment: "I

have quite forgiven him for that. I cannot bear him any ill-will."

"My husband is, unfortunately, capable of bearing ill-will, and for quite a while, too!"

At last, Djibi was able to leave her sickbed, though she dared not attempt jumping down from the chest. She sat near her bed, apprehensive, cowering, obviously not yet herself. The teacher caressed her fondly, talked gently to her. But Djibi behaved like a bad-tempered, distrustful stranger.

"Leave her alone," called Bertha. "She has only just come back from the dead."

The teacher wanted to take her in his arms and lift her down from the chest, but she resisted with such violence and hostility that it frightened him.

"What is the matter with you, puss? Are we no longer friends?"

He stood helplessly before her, lacking the courage to touch her again. "You are my darling puss; have you forgotten it?"

Djibi was not listening to him.

"What is wrong with her? Isn't she well yet?" He addressed his wife.

"She is far from well," replied Bertha. "She is still suffering from aftereffects."

"Poor, poor kitten," said the teacher compassionately.

"Yes, she is poor, and therefore she must be left in peace."

When Tasso came into the room and put his paws on the chest to greet Djibi, she arched her back and spat tonelessly.

Tasso was surprised, but did not try to force himself upon her. As she maintained her hostile attitude and continued to spit, the dog retreated in bewilderment.

"You see," observed Bertha. "She doesn't even recognize Tasso, and they were such close friends . . ."

"What will it all lead to?" whispered the teacher, bewildered.

"Everything will be well!" his wife consoled him. "But it takes time! You can't put it all straight overnight!

Isn't that so, pussy?" Her hand passed lightly over Djibi's back.

Djibi nestled closer to her nurse, and suddenly a low purring became audible.

"Did you hear that?" called Bertha to her husband.

"No!" he replied. "What was it?"

"Djibi has purred!"

The teacher wanted to take her in his arms again; but the cat, too weak to scratch, raised her paws in defense.

"I don't know what I have done!" The teacher turned away crossly. "I love animals as I have always done, and yet I fail in everything I try to do with them!"

"You must understand that she is still ill," reasoned Bertha.

"I must, I must . . ." he repeated querulously. "There is always a 'must' for me . . ."

"You must be considerate," interrupted Bertha.

"Does anyone trouble to be considerate to me?"

"You might remember your wife and Tasso."

In his cage, the canary began to warble a jubilant song.

After having listened to him for a time, enchanted, the teacher whispered: "Thank you. Thank you, little prisoner! You are happy, aren't you? You are a consolation and your song would warm anyone's heart!"

"At last, a pleasant word," murmured Bertha.

"You shall no longer be a prisoner," continued the teacher. "I am going to give you your freedom!"

"Don't for heaven's sake!" warned Bertha.

But the teacher had already opened the door of the cage.

The canary was silenced, appeared in the open door and peered round him. Then he flew flutteringly a short distance, sat down on the lampshade and twittered: "Peep!"

"How do you like it?" laughed the teacher.

"Peep!" replied the canary.

"Now sing!" insisted the teacher. "Sing a song of freedom!"

But the canary was silent. He seemed to appreciate neither his freedom nor his new position. He remained sitting on the lampshade.

"Shut the window!" ordered Bertha.

"Why?"

"Very well, I shall shut it myself!" Determined, she went to the window and fastened it securely.

"But Hansi should learn to know the trees and their green foliage . . ."

"Sometimes you are really stupid," she declared.

"Stupid?" he asked in surprise. "Because I want to give this bird its freedom?"

"I wish you would stop this freedom talk!" she interrupted him. "If Hansi got outside he would be completely helpless and the other birds would soon kill him!"

"Perhaps you're right," admitted the teacher.

"Of course I am right!" she cried impatiently. "I know you mean well, but you go about it the wrong way!"

The canary fluttered about in the room and landed on a chair.

Djibi lifted her head, pricked her eyes and eyed the bird with interest.

Bertha scolded, "What shall we do now? I suppose we shall have to chase him until he is exhausted, so that we may catch him again!"

"No!" begged the teacher. "No!"

"How else will he return to his house and get some peace?"

But Hansi spared the disconcerted teacher and supplied the answer himself. He flew over to his cage, sat for a while on its roof, called "Peep" several times, looked for the open door and slipped back into the familiar house, where he immediately began to peck at his seeds.

Bertha hurried to the cage, quickly climbed a chair and fastened the door. "There, that is far better for you than the much-praised liberty, of which you know nothing!"

Djibi's recovery was complete within a few weeks.

Still very thin, yet happy, she was her old self again.

When the teacher took her in his arms, she cuddled

up to him and purred like a spinning wheel.

He loved it when she mounted his shoulder and pressed her head under his chin, reciprocating his caresses.

The farmer, who came in and saw her, rubbed his hands contentedly: "Well, thank heavens!"

At the sight of him, Djibi took refuge with Bertha, to whom she had become extremely attached, in gratitude for her devoted nursing.

"Put her down on the floor," demanded the farmer.

"I'll do nothing of the sort," refused Bertha. "She is frightened of you, and with good cause."

Soon Djibi was well enough to walk about the room with her tail raised triumphantly.

Tasso greeted her fondly, and she renewed her friendship with the dog.

"Everything is settling down fine," rejoiced the teacher. "Patience is the main thing."

"And one shouldn't shirk any effort or give up hope," added his wife.

The teacher tried to justify himself.

"It is not surprising if at times I lost courage . . ."

"Oh, you!" Bertha patted his shoulder. "If things don't go the way you expect . . . If any of your illusions fail to become a reality, you immediately grow despondent, disappointed, a true pessimist! You ought to be ashamed of yourself!"

He smiled: "I am ashamed, and glad to acknowledge it!"

It gave Djibi obvious pleasure to parade about the room. Tasso accompanied her steps, wagging his tail gleefully.

Suddenly, he shot into a corner and growled. Djibi escaped into the teacher's lap.

The farmer entered the house.

"I saw Djibi walk about the room." He laughed. "Has the time come?"

"It has!" cried Bertha.

"Well, perhaps you'll talk to me now," said the farmer to the teacher, stretching out his hand.

The teacher took it, while Djibi sought Bertha's protection.

The farmer sighed with relief: "It has been a difficult time."

The teacher smiled: "But we were all lucky, you in particular!"

One morning, an imposing Persian tomcat sneaked into the room, examined every corner with composed curiosity, and finally sat down quietly at Djibi's side.

She received him with both dignity and a reserved amiability.

When he was greeted by the teacher and his wife, he showed gratitude, purred when he was stroked, but did not move, showing clearly that he wished to stay with Djibi.

"Well, stay then!" said the teacher.

Bertha warned the cat: "But you must behave when Tasso arrives! He will not hurt you, and we can't have any fights!"

The Persian looked at her as though he understood every word.

"What a fellow!" said Bertha. "He is a strapping big

creature, with a great deal of strength, and probably a temper, too. Who knows how he will take to the dog?..."

"At any rate, we must watch them," said the teacher.

He went up to the Persian and asked: "Do you agree to be called Rustan?"

At the word Rustan, the Persian lifted his head, pricked his ears and looked questioningly at the teacher.

Bertha laughed: "You seem to have guessed his name!"

"If I have, it's pure coincidence!" replied the teacher.

When Tasso came in the Persian leaped up, arched his back, and spat loudly.

"Hostilities have already begun!" cried the teacher's wife.

Tasso was taken aback at first, but then he approached very cautiously and slowly.

Djibi put her paw on the Persian's shoulder and seemed to explain something to him, which had the effect of calming him immediately; he crouched down and waited for the dog, though he was visibly nervous.

But Tasso's manner was so irresistably friendly that,

while it did not immediately win the Persian's affections, it compelled a peaceful attitude.

"That's good," smiled the teacher, contentedly. "At least there will be no fight. They will get on with each other."

Bertha was still doubtful. "Let's hope so."

"Good Tasso, good Rustan!" the teacher joined the animals, patting the dog and the cat. "If you could only tell me where you come from and why . . ."

The Persian listened attentively, and Tasso looked as though he had understood every word. He put his paw on the edge of the settee, and seemed to echo his master's question.

Djibi had stretched out coquettishly by their side. The Persian followed her and clapped her softly on the back, to which she responded with a contented "Mew."

"It is easy to guess *why* he has come," teased Bertha. "One need only look at our puss!"

But Rustan the Persian did not stay more than a few days with Djibi; another tomcat suddenly made his appearance. He was a very ordinary fellow, with shaggy fur and torn ears, which testified to many a bitter fight.

The teacher eyed him suspiciously. Bertha pitied him.

"A bad egg," was the teacher's verdict.

"A poor devil," said Bertha. "He must have had a hard time!"

"Only because of his unruly disposition," stated the teacher.

He was right, because the Ruffian immediately fell over Rustan, growling and spitting.

"What's all this?" intervened the teacher. "We must have peace here!"

But the newcomer took no notice of the teacher; he behaved as though he did not exist.

Intimidated, Rustan avoided the attack. But when the Ruffian threatened him again he jumped out of the window and escaped.

Bertha's eyes followed him: "We shall not see him again!"

"Coward!" muttered the teacher, annoyed.

But the Ruffian's rule did not last long either, though Djibi's attitude to him was most tender. The teacher and his wife left him alone, but could not love him. Tasso's reaction to the ill-mannered brute was different. At first he seemed dumbfounded, but then became so indignant that one day he suddenly seized the tomcat and threw him violently against the wall. The Ruffian was so taken aback that he made no sound, and lay quietly on the floor, stunned.

Tasso rushed at him and seemed ready to deal with him as he had dealt with the Angora cat.

"Tasso!" called the teacher in a subdued voice. "What are you doing?"

The dog immediately restrained himself obediently, wagged his tail and looked questioningly into the teacher's eyes.

"Don't be a murderer," warned the teacher softly.

Bertha supported him: "Tasso, don't ever make such a cruel exhibition again!"

The dog looked from the man to the woman, and

then looked at the cat in the corner, baring his fangs.

"Enough, old chap," said the teacher. "You have punished him sufficiently. Enough, now!"

"You are a good dog," praised Bertha.

The dog wagged his tail peaceably; then he lay down at the Ruffian's side, watching him closely. The Ruffian was recovering slowly.

The dog growled.

"He is not prepossessing," was the teacher's opinion of the Ruffian.

"I can't stand him either," admitted Bertha.

"But since he is staying with us," continued the teacher, "we must protect him."

"Of course," agreed Bertha. "But he mustn't always start a fight."

"He will get out of this habit."

"If he doesn't, he will have to bear the consequences. In that case, nobody can help him."

"These consequences worry me . . ."

"What must happen will happen, my dear, and all attempts to prevent it are useless!"

"Nevertheless, I shall do my best to see that peace reigns." The teacher did not give up hope.

The Ruffian got up cautiously, crept past the growling dog, and climbed up the settee, where he crouched at Djibi's side.

Djibi exerted all her charms to attract him; but he was too weary to take any notice of her. She sat pouting in the corner, but when the teacher took her in his arms, she immediately began to purr, took up her favorite position on his shoulder and behaved most lovingly.

"Pussy, sweet dear pussy," the teacher said tenderly.

The Ruffian spat.

"Be careful!" cried Bertha.

"Why? No animal will ever hurt me!"

"Don't be so confident! You never can know!"

The teacher repeated: "No animal will ever hurt me! Don't worry."

The words were hardly out of his mouth when the Ruffian was about to attack him. But Tasso leaped between the teacher and the cat, and the Ruffian cowered down again.

. . .

A little puppy attached himself to Tasso. He was young, playful, had no master and was pitifully starved. His urge to serve a master was even stronger than his hunger.

The puppy met with Tasso's approval.

He jumped up at the big dog, snapped at his ears, but Tasso tolerated him and behaved like a good-natured uncle.

Then the pup noticed Djibi and the Ruffian; he ran to them and poured out a stream of abuse. It was obvious that he was abusing them, because his voice sounded quite different; it was hostile, even threatening, entirely different from the voice with which he addressed Tasso.

Djibi completely ignored the little dog. She paid no attention to his barking, and did not even seem to consider him a nuisance.

The Ruffian, however, immediately arched his back and his claws hit out at the pup, who avoided him nimbly but grew more and more furious.

"What do you mean by all this noise?" asked the teacher.

The puppy was immediately silent, rolled on his back, full of boundless obedience and devotion.

Bertha, bending over him, was amused. "A funny chap! So young and so thin!"

"A child," said the teacher, to whom the pup appealed.

"A noisy child," smiled Bertha, "and a funny one!"

"He has the best instincts of his race," said the teacher approvingly. "Shall we keep him? You know that I am unable to turn away any animal."

"Of course I know it! I don't want to chase away the poor wretch."

"You have found the right name for the little chap. He shall be called 'Wretchy.'"

"All right. Wretchy, come with me and I'll teach you something more important than your name."

She fetched a bowl from the kitchen, filled with food to the brim. "You may have your meal in Tasso's company."

Tasso ate a few mouthfuls, indifferently. Wretchy sat impatiently on his hind legs, his head tilted to one side, pricking his ears, whining softly and trembling with greed.

Tasso raised his head, wagged his tail encouragingly and walked away.

"That's what I call an invitation!" approved Bertha.

"Of course," agreed the teacher. "Tasso is showing his hospitality, as usual."

"Come here, come here, Wretchy!" coaxed Bertha. "It is yours!" She whispered: "He can't possibly manage all that!"

But she had underestimated Wretchy. Like mad, he threw himself over the huge bowl: lap, lap, lap! He swallowed so passionately as though he had only just discovered the existence of food.

The entire meal, which would have satisfied the giant Tasso, disappeared in a jiffy. Little Wretchy had managed to eat it all. Then he sank down with a rounded belly, sighed deeply and immediately fell asleep.

Bertha shook her head. "It is incredible how much the little fellow managed to put away!"

"He had probably been starved for a long while, and

was generally leading a miserable existence," said the teacher.

A few days later Tasso liberated the household from Ruffian's shameless tyranny. The occasion for this deed was Wretchy, whom Tasso had to rescue from the Ruffian.

The pup was hopping playfully around the settee, on which the cats were lying.

Djibi surveyed his doings with the mien of a bored queen, disdainful of her subjects. But the Ruffian behaved differently. He arched his back, spat, and directed furious blows at the pup.

Tasso was stretched out on the floor. He had pricked his ears anxiously when Wretchy began his antics at the settee, because the Ruffian's attitude forecasted an attack.

The attack was not long in coming.

Wretchy continued to hop about, harmless and playful; from time to time he emitted a short, friendly bark, followed by a mad whirl through the room. He was quite engrossed in his game, and paid no attention to the Ruffian's menacing attitude.

The teacher had long ago made up his mind about

the Ruffian, and Tasso was equally candid in his disapproval of the cat.

"Take care, Tasso!" said the man to the dog. But the warning was unnecessary, because Tasso was keeping a careful watch.

Wretchy's happy barking was suddenly interrupted by a piercing yell of pain; the Ruffian had clawed him over the eyes, and the puppy, with his face bleeding, whining and bitterly disappointed, took refuge in Bertha's skirts.

Bertha cried indignantly: "That is too much!" She lifted Wretchy, washed his wound carefully, and tried to console the frightened little creature.

"I have seen it coming," said the teacher, equally indignant.

Tasso had risen. His angry growling sounded like low thunder.

Djibi leaped from the settee into the teacher's arms.

"She knows her friend," said Bertha, almost solemnly. "She knows that he's coming to administer justice and will show no mercy!"

"Be quiet, puss," the teacher whispered reassuringly. "Nothing will happen to you."

"You will only get rid of a bad tyrant," nodded Bertha.

The Ruffian faced the big, furious dog, alone.

He spat and hit out with his claws.

Tasso's wild roar resounded in the room; it expressed fury, hatred and threat. Then he snapped at the cat, caught him by the scruff of his neck and walked to the door, with the Ruffian shrieking and kicking helplessly in his iron grasp.

Bertha quickly opened the door. "That's right! Good dog!"

"But, Bertha!" said the teacher disapprovingly.

His wife ignored his remark and repeated: "That's right! That's right! Break the devil's neck!"

"How can you be like that?" complained the teacher, pressing Djibi tenderly to him. "We two, pussy, ask for nothing but peace, don't we?"

"I, too, want peace!" said the teacher's wife. "That is why this quarrelsome creature must be eliminated!"

In the meantime, Tasso had run out into the yard with his victim. The Ruffian's shrieks stopped. His fierce resistance came to an end. He lay semiconscious in Tasso's grip.

Tasso shook him so hard that everyone believed the Ruffian to be dead. He flung him violently to the ground, sniffed at his inert body but seized him again at the slightest movement, gave him a renewed shaking and dropped him again.

Bertha, who had stepped out of the door, cried: "Enough, enough, Tasso!"

Tasso looked obliquely at the Ruffian and wagged his tail.

The teacher came out, too; he was holding Djibi in his arms, examined the tomcat and declared, with satisfaction: "He has not killed him! He has spared his life. Good dog, good Tasso!"

Tasso ran to him, wagging with delight, a victor, yet without pride. He received the patting of his praising master with gratitude. Bertha looked on, while Wretchy jumped about her fussily, his recent pain forgotten.

The Ruffian seemed to have lost all his fighting spirit. He rose unsteadily and tried to sneak his way back to the house.

But Tasso stopped him by standing in his way and barking furiously. Wretchy joined in eagerly with his thin, high-pitched yapping.

The Ruffian turned back, intimidated, and dragged himself wearily across the yard.

Tasso followed him with a growling bark, accompanied by the yapping puppy.

Pursued by his enemies, the Ruffian deemed it advisable to hurry a little; he found it difficult, but succeeded, nevertheless. They chased him as far as the gate, which led to the road, and every time the Ruffian made an attempt to edge away from them toward the house, Tasso showed clear signs of his mounting rage.

Twice the tomcat tried to turn back, and failed. Dejectedly, he realized the futility of his attempts, crossed the road and disappeared into the fields, not to be seen again.

Tasso stood guard for a while at the gate, then he withdrew into the yard, satisfied.

The teacher and his wife had watched the proceedings anxiously and hopefully.

The man gave a sigh of relief: "Thank heavens, no murder and no bloodshed! Tasso has behaved grandly."

Bertha replied, laughingly. "Yes, I am pleased about it, too. But you must admit that it has been a true expulsion of Satan."

A very young tomcat sought Djibi's favor. He was ingenious and full of fun, had white spotted fur and his gestures were attractive in their clumsy playfulness.

Djibi received him with obvious delight; she immediately displayed her alluring coquettishness.

"A child," said the teacher. "A true child!"

The young tomcat wooed Djibi charmingly, and she teased him.

Bertha shook her head. "So young and already so much in love! Men are really wicked."

"Well," said the teacher, "anyone who knows puss

and who has seen the number of lovers to whom she has given herself indiscriminately cannot have a very high opinion of women, either."

The young tomcat stayed. He met with Tasso's approval, who liked rolling him gently on the ground; Spots willingly entered into the spirit of the game.

Wretchy was also delighted with him and loved him with the warm devotion of youth. Spots did not always lounge on the settee with Djibi. On the contrary, he always responded to the puppy's invitation to play. The two then rolled about on the floor, their limbs entangled.

Djibi did not wish to remain a lone spectator of these youthful frolics. She slipped down from the settee, took part in their jolly games and before long became their acknowledged leader.

She was so gay and lively with them that she showed neither fear nor a desire to escape when the farmer came in.

Only Tasso growled at the sight of the farmer, but he, too, quieted down when he saw him shake hands with the teacher.

"Hullo!" exclaimed the farmer. "Your place sounds pretty jolly!"

"It is," laughed Bertha. "That's how we like it!"

Wretchy, who was not disturbed by evil memories, jumped friskily at the farmer's legs and wagged his tail violently.

The farmer stretched out his hand and said, in surprise: "You *are* a nice dog!" stroking him clumsily as he spoke.

Wretchy lay on his back, with an expression of utter devotion, and then whirled like mad through the room in appreciation of the caresses he had received.

The farmer laughed. "I must say I like the little fellow!"

He stretched out his hand to stroke Tasso too; the dog submitted to him after having been reassured by a glance from his master, but could not suppress a low growl. The teacher whispered: "Be good, Tasso!" and the growling stopped, but Tasso did not wag his tail.

"Be good!" repeated the farmer shyly. "The two of us will be friends again!"

"Do you understand now what pleasure one can derive from animals?"

"I do!" laughed the farmer. "I do, indeed! One always learns something new from you."

"But you learn slowly and reluctantly!" said Bertha. "You're just a farmer . . ."

"Of course, I'm a farmer, and a good one at that! I have no time for your highbrow stuff."

"Nevertheless, you have proved yourself that in your station, too, one can find time for what you call 'highbrow stuff,'" Bertha contradicted him.

"And you even realize that it does you a lot of good," added the teacher.

"Maybe! But I will not permit anyone to insult or ridicule the farmers!"

The teacher came quite close to him. "Don't ever say that again! Nobody here would dream of insulting or ridiculing the farmers. Do you understand? Nobody!"

"All right, all right!" said the farmer, abashed. "I only meant to say . . ."

Bertha interrupted him: "My dear fellow, when I refer to your personal stupidity it is by no means a reflection upon the farmer class as a whole. Remember that!"

The animals were asleep.

Bertha and the teacher sat on a bench outside their door. Tasso lay at their feet.

The deep nocturnal sky was starlit. It was a pleasure and a relief to inhale the mild summer evening air.

Both were silent for a long time. There was reverence in their silence. Then the teacher whispered:

"The music of the spheres . . . can you hear it?"

"I can feel it," replied Bertha softly.

Again the teacher's whispering voice: "This music must always have been there, but men had no ear for it . . ."

After a short pause, Bertha asked: "What exactly do you mean?"

"My dear, I am convinced that things must have happened that way!"

"Which way?"

"Well, in ancient times all men spoke a single language and understood each other, until they took it into their heads . . ."

"Are you referring to the tower of Babel?"

"Yes."

"It was a great idea . . ."

"But a still greater impudence! They wanted to penetrate into the heavens, to see God and his legions . . ."

"Unfortunately, they did not succeed!"

"No, my dear! The Almighty frowned upon their audacity. And He can be very furious!"

"Are you being blasphemous?"

"Nothing is further from my mind than blasphemy. I am only trying to understand the Creator!"

"You are building a tower of Babel in your thoughts!"

"The Creator cannot possibly frown upon that. He is not only all-powerful, but also kind, and He has endowed us with the capacity for thought."

"And yet He can be furious! You have said so yourself."

"I did not say so, Bertha. The incident is related in the Holy Scriptures, which I am merely trying to interpret."

"Go on!"

"Because mankind had impudently tried to intrude upon Him, and because He was seized by fury, He confused men by making them speak different tongues. They no longer understood each other. They became strangers, and then enemies. With the end of mutual understanding, mistrust, strife and war made their entrance into the world."

"And what happened then?"

"Then, my dear, happened the greatest miracle of the Creation, which revealed God's boundless benevolence and mercy. When God saw the consequences of His fury, when He realized that the harm caused by the difference of languages could not be undone, He sent His angels down to teach men a language which would be understood by all, which would penetrate into their souls, grip their hearts and purify their minds: Music!"

"Yes, this conciliatory bond is truly divine!"

"Isn't it? We must listen to the harmony of Nature and hear God's message in the voice of a solitary canary warbling merrily in his cage."

Djibi completely abandoned her favorite place on the settee. As before, she wandered through the yard and the fields beyond, followed by the young tomcat and accompanied by the always gay, always dancing, Wretchy.

"I don't like her to go so often into the fields," worried the teacher.

"She will come to no harm."

"Who knows?"

"Would you like to keep pussy in a glass house?"

"She would certainly be safest there."

"She is only out on mouse hunting. Spots and Wretchy are with her."

"Those two can hardly be regarded as protectors."

"She is no longer in need of protection. She needs company. It revives and rejuvenates her."

· · ·

One evening Tasso arrived carrying Djibi in his teeth. She appeared completely inert.

"Tasso!" cried the teacher, alarmed.

The dog barked at him, then he put the cat on the floor, where she suddenly came to life and began stalking about.

Bertha was amused. "It is her old custom. Why get alarmed? You are too nervous, my dear."

"Perhaps. Nervous with the constant worry and anxiety . . . How easy it is for the cat to get hurt or even killed!"

"It is no longer necessary to watch and worry over pussy so much."

"You forget, Bertha, what we went through, and what pussy had to suffer. I shall always remember it."

"But all this is happily over now. You ought to be grateful!"

Shortly afterward, a rat ran across the yard, big and fat.

Wretchy was the first to see her, and began to dance around her foolishly, thereby forcing her to run in different directions all the time.

Djibi shot out of the house, observed the confused course of the rat and ducked, ready to pounce on her prey. In that position she was wonderfully like a lioness.

Then a well-timed leap. The rat squeaked, but before she could squeak again Djibi had seized her by the neck and bitten through her throat. She shook the dead body briefly, threw it down and turned away with obvious signs of utter disgust. As she walked away with dignified composure, her attitude seemed to indicate that she had merely administered justice.

Wretchy trotted friskily at her side, a much impressed worshipper of victory.

The young tomcat, too, circled round her and expressed his jolly admiration in many gay pranks.

Djibi avoided with firm friendliness the teacher's attempts to caress her; she jumped on a bench and began to attend to her toilet with great care.

"Leave her alone," smiled Bertha. "She feels impure through her contact with the rat . . . she must clean herself."

The teacher fetched a spade and buried the dead rat.

In the meantime Djibi ran out into the street, followed, of course, by her attendants.

"She mustn't do that!" cried the teacher, and hurried anxiously to the gate. "Come back, pussy!"

Bertha tapped him on the shoulder. "You had better come in. It is no use calling or waiting. Cats have no sense of obedience, as well you know!"

"I demand no obedience! But out of friendship she should respond to my call!"

"My dear, she wants to be out now! And she must have her way. But wait a minute! We can get her back." She called "Tasso! Fetch pussy! Quickly!"

The dog set out galloping and brought Djibi back after a short time, in his usual way. The young tomcat and Wretchy accompanied his entry.

They had hardy all got into the yard when a lorry could be heard rattling in the road outside. The farmer was sitting at the wheel. He stopped and switched off the engine. "That's a surprise for you, what? I got the old thing very cheap. Now I can take my harvest into town quickly, and earn more! It will have paid for itself before the year is out."

"Good luck!" called the teacher.

"Thank you!" grinned the farmer. "I can always do with good luck!"

He started the lorry again, and after some hesitation the engine decided to do its duty.

"It saves the horses, too!" he shouted, but the din of the motor rendered his words almost inaudible. He waved and drove off.

"A capable fellow," said Bertha approvingly.

"Hard-working and assiduous," agreed the teacher.

"I am sure he will grow rich . . ."

"You mean he will grow richer, because he is rich already."

In the evening the teacher and his wife sat in front of the house, in the light of the full moon.

Djibi, the young tomcat and Wretchy all slept together on the settee.

Tasso lay stretched out at his master's feet.

"We couldn't afford a car, could we?" said the teacher jokingly.

"Do you need one?" asked Bertha. Her tone was disdainful.

"Oh, no! I have no desire for one!" replied the teacher soothingly.

"I know what you mean, my dear. You want to say that we are richer than the farmer."

"You are quite right, Bertha, that is what I meant!"

"Today I can again feel Nature's wonderful music."

"Moonshine music, isn't it?"

"Yes, a soft, lovely music . . . an enchantment, my dear . . ."

"A comforting, moving, exalting enchantment, Bertha."

"I can feel it, too. The night has a message of hope, but also one of sadness."

"A foreboding, the certainty of death . . . isn't it so?"

"Perhaps . . . I don't want to think about it. And yet it weighs heavily on my heart."

"Pity with ourselves . . ."

"Maybe . . . but even more so with God's dumb creatures. To think they are all dumb! It always moves me, and compels me to love them."

"They all have their own language, my child."

"But not ours, my dear, and we have no access to theirs."

"And yet we can understand each other."

"But the understanding is only very, very limited."

"We must be satisfied with it, Bertha."

"But it is by no means sufficient! Do we know what pussy felt when she was ill-treated by the farmer? She may have blamed you for it! If we could only know..."

"Heaven knows, Bertha, we always come up against the blank wall which separates us from our dumb brothers. It's fate! I never feel so impotent in the impact with this blank wall as when an animal is suffering."

"I feel the wall most painfully when I take action against any animal. I have often asked myself whether I have not done the Ruffian an injustice..."

"Don't worry about the Ruffian, my child. Let him be your guide!" The teacher pointed down to Tasso.

"And the rat? Why are we so hard on rats?"

"There are animals, Bertha, which remain alien and hostile to human beings, just as there are others who serve them quietly and submissively, such as cattle, and who would even serve them better if they were treated with more kindness and consideration. I include pigs in their number. A rat may possibly be capable of forming some kind of friendship with a prisoner in his cell, but otherwise . . ."

"How many strange possibilities . . ."

"I will remind you of the spider, Bertha, which is repulsive to most people, because they do not know that spiders are very intelligent, and under certain circumstances, quite tame. The same applies to some serpents, of course not the poisonous ones . . . I once knew an exceptional boy who, unfortunately, died very young. One day he brought an aesculapius adder into the house. Where did he get it? asked his father. From a pet shop. Why? Because she was so lonely there! The boy kept the serpent in his room, and waited for an opportunity to let her free in the mountains. On one occasion the family had a guest for dinner, and the conversation turned to the serpent. The guest was curious to see her, and the boy brought her out and put her on the dining table after it had been cleared. She remained still for a while and then began to creep about as if in search of something. The guest stretched out his hand. She shot at it, hissed and turned resolutely away. She also turned away from the father's hand, but immediately recognized the boy's and crawled over his arm right up to the shoulder. She then crawled back and remained lying content-edly with her beautiful head resting in the palm of his hand."

"How strange and yet how explicable! Though we human beings have been driven out of the Garden of Eden, some of us have, nevertheless, retained certain instincts and tendencies which I would call fragmentary remnants. The desire for the companionship of animals, the brotherly feelings toward these creatures . . ."

The teacher looked at his wife with some sur-prise. After a short while he sighed: "Very fragmentary feelings . . . they prompt us to try and develop our friendship with animals."

Bertha laughed heartily: "They are remnants, remember! It is the same in the case of those animals who are affectionately disposed toward human beings. Their fraternal feelings are also only a fragmentary remnant of distant, better days."

He sighed again. "The better days always seem to us distant and in the past. They may be no more than the dreams of our longing, our never satisfied longing."

Bertha put an end to these meditations. "No more brooding!" she declared with determination. "It does not do any good to dwell upon these things. What can come of it? It is nothing but groping and erring in the dark."

"You're quite right, my dear. But something drives us on . . ."

"Don't let yourself be pushed and driven!"

"What else can I do?"

"Nothing, you blind scholar! Things are as they are, and we must say: 'They are fine!' We can say it with a good conscience!"

"Really, Bertha? With a good, clear conscience?"

"Yes! We don't stint our efforts! We do whatever is in our power . . ."

"You have called me a blind scholar . . ."

"My poor dear, all scholars are blind, but they want to see. The urge for light is characteristic of the blind; the urge to see marks the scholar."

"Perhaps there is some truth in this way of thinking . . ."

"I hope you don't think I am doing wrong . . . that is the last thing I want."

"No, my dear. There can be no question of right or wrong between us."

"What, then, is the question?"

"Whether there is concord between us."

"Dearest, in a large forest of oak trees you will not find two leaves which are completely identical."

"What do you imply thereby, Bertha?"

"We are as identical as possible. Our roots are the same, we agree on all vital matters. We must be content with that."

"I am more than content with it! It is a supreme and rare happiness."

"Thank you for feeling that way . . ."

"Don't thank me! I don't deserve it."

"Very well, dear. I will not thank you. I'll thank the Almighty for having brought us together."

Djibi and the young tomcat were lovers.

At night, strange tomcats screeched, groaned and sang in all keys in front of the house.

The young tomcat wanted to go out. He trembled with eagerness to fight.

But Djibi stopped him, and he gave in.

Sometimes Tasso would rush into the yard, followed by Wretchy. The two soon put an end to the cats' orchestra.

Tasso's appearance was in itself sufficient to scatter them, and Wretchy assisted him with excited yapping and chasing.

Djibi suddenly grew gentler, softer, more tender. She delighted the teacher because she never tired of his caresses. But one day she began to resist the advances of her hitherto beloved tomcat.

Bertha, in whose arms she lay purring, felt her body and declared:

"Pussy is pregnant!"

"Now we must take care that Tasso doesn't drag her about in his teeth," said the teacher.

"That won't hurt her!" contradicted his wife.

"At any rate, she must no longer go into the fields, and, above all, not into the road!"

But Djibi ran into the fields as before, hunting mice, strayed in the road and was brought home by Tasso as usual.

In vain did the teacher always protest against her escapades. Djibi proved as affectionate as she was self-willed, charming, but disobedient.

When the time of her confinement drew near, she hardly left the house. She walked about the room restlessly, and looked appealingly at the teacher and at his wife in turn.

She kept the young tomcat and the frisky, playful

puppy at arm's length, and they soon left her alone. Tasso was the only one whose proximity she tolerated. Their friendship withstood any crisis.

One day she followed Bertha at every step, wailing plaintively and impatiently. Bertha bent down to her and laid her hand on the cat's head.

Djibi pressed her forehead against this hand, emitted a piercing shriek and gave birth to a kitten.

"Any more coming, puss?" inquired the teacher with concern.

But no more came.

The newly-born had no life in it. Djibi nevertheless attended to it with the most tender maternal care, licked, cleaned and nursed her child, which never moved. Finally she put the kitten to her breast. It then appeared that she had no milk to suckle it.

Djibi made innumerable attempts to revive the poor little creature, but in vain. It was dead in less than an hour.

But Djibi did not give in. She could neither believe that her child had died, nor resign herself to the fact.

While the teacher held her in his arms, speaking tender words to her, while Bertha disposed of the kitten and buried it, Djibi pulled more and more violently away from her protector.

When he at last released her, she jumped down to the ground and began to search for the kitten.

She searched everywhere, whining all the time with a thin voice.

Strangely enough, Wretchy kept very still as he was watching her. The young tomcat, too, as though conscience-stricken, did not move a limb; he lay timidly on the settee, while Djibi searched and searched, and her low complaint was the only sound to be heard in the room. She turned to Tasso, to his master, and her eyes spoke the question: "Where is my child?" and the entreaty, "Give it back to me!"

The teacher, deeply moved, said: "It is a tragedy!"

Bertha, always less sentimental, shrugged her shoulders.

"Do you know what goes on in a cat's head? She will soon forget!"

But, in spite of Bertha's forecast, Djibi's memories lived on. She stopped searching after a time, but remained listless. She wailed a great deal, seemed to expect from the teacher and his wife the restitution of her child, and grew estranged from them as her expectation remained unfulfilled.

The teacher, who watched Djibi's transformation anxiously, said repeatedly: "It's a tragedy!"

Bertha again put forward the argument that cats have short memories, but he replied: "You may be right where daily matters are concerned. This, however, touches the root of life, the essence of existence. It cannot be subject to definite rules."

"Let's wait and see," said Bertha.

The young tomcat, Djibi and Wretchy were playing together in the yard. Again a rat hurried by.

The young tomcat jumped at her, though he was hardly as big as she, and certainly not as fat.

The rat put up a stiff defense, and bit him hard, so that he released his grip with a cry of pain and surprise.

But Djibi had already arrived to his rescue. She seized the rat unerringly by the neck, bit right through her throat before she could even squeak, shook the dead body and flung it away in disgust, just as she had done with the first rat.

The young tomcat was bleeding rather profusely. He whined pitifully and ran frightened into the house.

"I hope the rat bite will have no ill-effects," said the teacher, who had witnessed the incident and felt worried.

"Why always anticipate the worst?" objected Bertha.

"A rat bite can easily lead to blood-poisoning."

"The little chap can stand it."

But the young tomcat could not stand it. The wound would not heal, and he lost his liveliness. At first it was not very noticeable. Yet the teacher, who watched him closely, grew anxious.

"Bertha, I don't like the look of the little one."

"What's the matter? I can see no cause for alarm."

"I am sure there is something very wrong with him."

"You exaggerate, as usual."

"I hope you are right, Bertha, but I fear for his life because of the rat bite."

The young cat licked his wounds. Gradually he became quite listless. When Djibi invited him to play, he did not move, but only pawed her weakly.

Then he stopped cleaning himself, and his fur grew bristly and lusterless.

Now Djibi began to avoid him; she even seemed to fear him.

"Bertha, can't you see the change in the little one?"

"I'm not blind . . ."

"It's certainly a consequence of the rat bite . . ."

"Ridiculous!"

"But there can be no other reason."

"If you're so worried, send for the vet!"

They did, and the vet came. He was a young, hearty man, and obviously very kind.

"What is the matter? Who is the patient?" he inquired immediately upon entering.

The teacher explained the case.

"Nothing serious," ventured Bertha.

"We shall have to see," said the doctor; "from what I hear, it is not quite so simple."

It was difficult to hold the young tomcat during his examination. He tried to bite and scratch the doctor's hand, but the latter handled him so capably and soothed him so well that he soon ceased to resist.

The doctor examined the wound carefully. Then he shrugged his shoulders. "There is nothing much I can do. Blood-poisoning! He may overcome the poison, but I doubt it. If you like . . . I'll relieve him immediately. The animal will be spared any further suffering, and it takes a bare second."

Bertha said with determination: "If that is the case, do it. It's best for the cat."

"No!" opposed the teacher. "You did say, doctor, that he may overcome the poison . . ."

"It is possible, but, as I have said, very doubtful."

"Still, you admit the possibility?" asked the teacher, agitated.

"I cannot exclude a faint chance."

"I'll take it," decided the teacher. "Who knows? Cats are tough!"

The doctor left. The young tomcat continued to lick his wound. But it would not heal.

Djibi still kept away from him.

"It is awful to watch his tortures," said Bertha. "I wish you had agreed to put an end to him . . ."

"As long as there is life there is hope," warned her husband.

"You can hardly call it life any longer. At most it is a weary death-struggle."

A few days later the young tomcat disappeared. His masters searched for him everywhere, but could not find him.

Tasso had to be appealed to.

"Where is the young tomcat?" asked the teacher.

"Find him!" urged Bertha.

The dog sniffed eagerly all round the room, sniffed at all the corners, but was visibly frightened when he put his nose under the cupboard.

"That's where the little one is," said the teacher.

"And he is no longer alive," added Bertha sadly.

"How do you know?"

"Didn't you notice how frightened Tasso was? It's an infallible sign."

They pushed the cupboard aside; the young cat lay there, stretched out. He had hidden himself away to die.

The wound inflicted by the rat bite gaped wide open, its edges were swollen.

Djibi seemed quite indifferent; she showed no signs of missing her former gay playmate.

She often ran out into the fields to chase mice and, with a stubbornness nobody could understand, insisted on sitting in the middle of the road.

Tasso always had to be sent out to fetch her, which he did, invariably accompanied by the faithful Wretchy.

Then Djibi would purr in the teacher's lap, climb up to his shoulder, push her head under his chin and unfold all her tenderness.

"God's creatures are modest," said the teacher to his

wife, delighted. "All they want is our tender kindness, and they are ready to love us for it!"

"Poor little thing!" said Bertha, who was thinking of the young tomcat. "He would have grown up into a charming creature."

"Yes, it's a great pity."

A few peaceful weeks went by.

Then Bertha said one evening: "I am very worried about Wretchy."

"About this jolly chap?"

"Yes, because he is no longer jolly since yesterday."

The canary sang in his cage. His warbling inspired the teacher with confidence and good humor.

"What is the matter with Wretchy?"

"He slinks about dejectedly and won't touch his food."

"Some little trouble! Tummy-ache! Dogs have it too!"

"Tasso never had any."

"Well, our Tasso! He is a giant, not only by stature, and his constitution cannot be compared to that of poor little Wretchy."

"Look at the puppy! He is certainly ill."

The frisky puppy was indeed ill.

On the following morning he did not get up at all, but lay on one side, with glassy eyes and a dry, hot nose.

"Fever!" said Bertha. "High fever!"

The teacher approached: "Oh, dear, distemper!"

Djibi abandoned the puppy. She refused to remain next to him on the settee.

"What can I do to help you, you poor thing?" wailed Bertha.

"I'll call the vet," promised the teacher. "He will find ways and means."

The vet concluded, after a very brief examination: "A serious case of distemper. Hardly a hope."

He took out his syringe. "It would be best to relieve him of his suffering now."

The teacher resisted: "Even a feeble glimmer of hope still means hope."

The vet smiled, derisively: "Just as you like! But I can't see the faintest glimmer."

Soon afterward Wretchy's hind legs became para-lyzed.

"This is the beginning of the end," said the vet.

"I can't stand it any longer!" cried Bertha. "Put an end to it, doctor!"

The teacher did not dare to intervene.

And so the vet pricked Wretchy's breast with the death needle, saying: "The puppy is more dead than alive, anyhow."

Wretchy did not even show signs of convulsion. Everything was over immediately.

The teacher turned away. He could not restrain his tears and sobbed quietly.

"There, there!" his wife tried to calm him. "I, too, grieve for the little fellow, but where there is no help . . . Think of the human beings who have to suffer to the bitter end because it is forbidden to offer them this last mercy."

The farmer had heard of Wretchy's death and came to offer his condolences.

"What a shame," he sighed, but it was impossible to tell whether he was sincere or not. The teacher and his wife therefore remained silent.

The farmer, however, did not budge; he sniffed, blew his nose, and looked dejectedly in front of him. Finally he said, after a great effort of thinking: "Yes, he was such a nice dog..."

He wished them to believe in his sorrow.

As there was still no answer, he grew secretly hostile again.

"You see, Teacher, one should never make any resolutions, since it is impossible to keep them..."

Bertha asked sharply: "What exactly do you mean?"

"Oh, nothing!" he replied eagerly. "Only... it is true, isn't it, that you had the poor little puppy put to sleep?"

"Certainly!" affirmed Bertha. "There was no hope for him, so we released him from his pain."

The farmer shook his head: "I would never have believed it of you!"

Bertha snapped at him crossly: "What's this nonsense you're talking?"

"It's no nonsense! I know what I'm talking about, and the teacher knows it quite well, too!"

"Perhaps you will admit me into your confidence as well?" she inquired coldly.

"Didn't you affirm, Teacher, that you would never kill an animal?"

"But I've explained to you . . ." Bertha tried again.

"It makes no difference!" interrupted the farmer. "You were very proud of yourself for never killing an animal under any circumstances!"

"Listen to me, Farmer!"

"There is no need for me to listen! You can't deny that you were responsible for killing the little dog. Nor can you deny that you were proud of your principles, but that you have, nevertheless, acted against them."

The teacher left the room without a word, slamming the door behind him.

The sun poured warmth over the house, the yard and the fields. The pigeons walked about, cooing. The birdcage stood on the windowsill and Hansi warbled long, melodious tunes. Djibi lay stretched out on a sunny spot on the floor, and Tasso kept a tender watch over her.

The teacher sat comfortably in his chair, and Bertha busied herself quietly between the room and the kitchen.

It was a lovely, peaceful day.

Suddenly a magpie flew into the room, chatted a little and behaved as though she were an old acquaintance and had always lived there.

Djibi only raised her head, looked at the newcomer curiously but without surprise, and continued sunning herself.

Tasso walked up to the magpie and amicably wagged his stump of a tail.

"The master of ceremonies," smiled the teacher.

Bertha asked in astonishment: "Where on earth does she come from?"

"I haven't the faintest idea, my dear wife!"

With her head cocked to one side, the magpie tiptoed to Djibi and pecked gently at her.

Djibi's paw hit out lazily, but missed the bird, who fluttered back and emitted a deep call, which sounded like "Ohe!"

The magpie returned to Djibi almost immediately, and poked her beak into Djibi's flank.

This time the cat shot up.

But the magpie flew buzzingly across the room, and settled on the lamp, calling out again: "Ohe!"

The teacher and his wife watched her as she sat up there surveying the room with intelligent eyes.

"What an elegant bird," said the teacher.

"A clever bird," agreed Bertha. "But don't let us forget that she steals. You know the saying: 'Thievish as a magpie!'"

"Since we have nothing of value, my dear, there is no harm in her stealing."

Bertha wondered: "I can't think what she has come for . . ."

"Company," replied the teacher. "Entertainment, play . . . just look at her!"

Djibi and Tasso were looking up at the lamp, full of anticipation.

The magpie chatted away. It almost sounded as if she were laughing.

Suddenly she fluttered down and flew at Djibi.

Tasso stood in front of Djibi in order to protect her.

But the magpie did no harm: she behaved in a nice and playful manner.

Tasso and Djibi were only partly amused; they were partly suspicious, as though expecting an attack.

To everybody's surprise, the magpie settled on Tasso's back, and began pecking at his head.

Tasso shook himself violently. This upset the bird's balance and she fluttered down toward the floor, but flew up again, obviously because Djibi was standing by with raised paws, ready to catch her.

The magpie kept fluttering up and down, rose to the ceiling and came down to the floor.

She seemed to be teasing.

Tasso alternately raised and lowered his head,

following her movements with amazement.

Djibi vainly tried to catch the bird. The magpie returned to the lamp, where she took a seat.

"Ohe!" she called in a deep voice, then laughed.

"This bird will come to a bad end," feared Bertha.

"Why so?" contradicted her husband. "They are only playing with each other!"

"I have no objection," said Bertha, "but I doubt whether they will go on playing all the time. I think there will be some trouble soon."

At first the teacher's view seemed to prevail, but when the farmer arrived the situation became critical.

The magpie refused to tolerate his presence in the room.

At first he treated her attacks jocularly.

"One always meets strange creatures at your place," he remarked.

"Isn't she lovely?" smiled Bertha.

"She would be lovely if she gave me some peace," he said, trying to ward off the bird.

But the magpie attacked him with increased violence.

He hit out at her with his cap, but she escaped him nimbly, fluttered onto his shoulder and stabbed his cheek with her beak.

He gave a forced laugh: "Stop it, it hurts!"

But the magpie would not let go and pressed still closer to him.

He hit out with his cap again, and demanded: "Teacher, call this vulture off!"

The teacher was amused. "This bird won't obey me! And it isn't a vulture, only a magpie."

The farmer turned his head right and left, but in vain.

"Ohe!" said the magpie, suddenly in her full voice.

The farmer was quite startled. "You damned creature!" he cried angrily. "The devil take you!" he shouted again, as the magpie grew still bolder and dug her beak more and more vigorously into his face.

"Look here!" he roared at least, "if you refuse to help me, I'll leave!"

"I would like to help you," said the teacher, "but how can I? I don't know the bird!"

"It's no good trying to fib to me! I know you're on terms of intimacy with all animals!"

Perhaps the farmer's loud and angry voice provoked the magpie; her attacks increased and became unbearable.

"Things have come to a pretty pass when you allow a bird to drive me out!" grumbled the farmer as he made for the door.

"I assure you I'm not responsible!" called the teacher. But the farmer did not hear him. He was already gone.

"Some animals have sound instincts," said Bertha, laughing.

Djibi climbed deftly up to the teacher's shoulder.

"Coming back home, puss?"

She pressed her head under his chin and purred.

He stroked her gently, delighted. "Dear, dear puss . . ."

But she did not stay long; one leap brought her down to the floor, and she whisked out through the open door.

"Where are you hurrying to, puss?"

Djibi paid no attention to his question.

As the teacher stood outside the front door, he saw her run toward the fields.

"Let her be," said Bertha. "She is out on a mouse hunt."

"I wish that were all . . . but she always goes into the street afterward."

"Send Tasso for her! He'll get her back."

"Tasso!"

The dog arrived eagerly, wagged his stumpy tail and pricked his ears attentively.

"Fetch pussy, Tasso!"

The dog departed promptly on his mission.

He stayed away a long time. At last, the teacher, who was waiting impatiently outside the house, saw Tasso arrive from the street, with Djibi in his mouth.

"In the street again!" he said, very displeased. "Heaven only knows why the cat is so attracted to the street!"

Djibi continued to prowl about. In the fields, in the street, and also in the farmer's yard, where she stole a rabbit again.

The farmer, who immediately discovered her misdeed, came to accuse the cat.

"You see," said the teacher, "that is the proper way to act. Now we can settle the matter in a decent way."

"Will you pay me damages? You know you said you would!"

"Of course I'll pay! I am in the habit of keeping my word. How much?"

The farmer named a sum, which the teacher was about to pay without bargaining, when Bertha intervened.

"You mustn't take advantage of us like that! For that amount I can get three rabbits. You're only entitled to the usual price!"

They agreed on a figure; the teacher held Djibi in his arms while Bertha paid.

"Is this a nice thing to do, puss?" he talked softly to her. "Don't we give you enough to eat?" But Djibi tore away from him and ran out.

Soon afterward she could be heard screaming in the field.

Tasso was already on his way to her.

"Help her!" cried the teacher. The dog rushed off.

A huge tomcat had attacked Djibi and was about to maul her badly.

She turned and wriggled under his unfriendly wooing. She scratched and bit him furiously, but as he was the stronger, he would undoubtedly have damaged her seriously before he had his way.

At this juncture Tasso arrived to her rescue, seized the dangerous suitor and flung him away.

The tomcat remained lying motionless on the ground.

Tasso's murderous teeth had bitten right through his neck.

Djibi crawled up to the dead body, sniffed at it and wailed plaintively.

Tasso stood by, dumbfounded, looking from Djibi to the dead cat. He couldn't understand what had happened; he had meant well and was mystified at Djibi's sorrow.

"Don't grieve, pussy," said the teacher, who had followed Tasso and picked Djibi up, fondling her. "You will never lack suitors."

But Djibi did not purr, nor did she wish to stay in his arms. She leaped down and disappeared before he had time to stop her.

This time peril overtook her.

She had resumed her attacks on the rabbits, and grew wilder as her lust to kill increased.

The farmer knew it, and waited for her as he saw her coming.

He took up his post behind a tall threshing machine. All sorts of farming implements were scattered there, a ploughshare, several spades, a heavy spare wheel of the lorry.

The farmer's eye took stock of all these articles, with no other intention than to frighten Djibi and chase her away should she steal up to the rabbit hutch again. He only meant to clap his hands, or possibly rattle with the spade.

But when he saw Djibi stalking up to the rabbits, he flew into a blind rage.

The teacher would have found her supple tiger step and her lion attitude enchanting. In the farmer, however, it provoked suddenly such violent fury that he did what he least intended. He seized the first thing he could lay hands on, and threw the ploughshare at her.

The cold steel hit Djibi with such force that it smashed her spine.

She collapsed with a stifled cry. The heavy piece of metal tipped over and fell over the cat, killing her after a brief death struggle.

The farmer grew pale as he hurried to her.

Subconsciously, he felt a revengeful satisfaction. He had hated Djibi from the first. But his dread of the teacher and his wife was stronger than any other feeling.

Tasso, who had been sent to look for Djibi, drew back in terror from his dead friend, and began to mourn for her with loud, long wails. He did not budge from her side, and howled persistently until the teacher and his wife came running by.

"So you have been her destruction, after all!" cried Bertha, while the farmer stammered: "It really isn't my fault . . ."

"No," said the teacher bitingly. "You are innocent!

The poor creature has deliberately thrown herself under the ploughshare!"

The farmer repeated, stammering: "It isn't my fault…"

The teacher eyed him sternly from head to foot: "Listen to me, man! From now on we are complete strangers, remember that! Don't ever let me set eyes on you again!"

With these words, he turned away. "Let's go, Bertha! Come, Tasso, or something might happen to you of which this fellow is innocent!"

On their way home with the dead cat, the teacher sighed bitterly. "My poor, dear, pussy!"

Bertha consoled him. "It's all for the best," she said. "Pussy was well on her way to lose her mind. Believe me, she would have had rabies before long!"

The teacher was so despondent that he was willing to believe anything.

The farmer remained behind, alone, scratched his head and murmured: "Once a fool, always a fool! All this fuss for a measly cat!"